E R A S E D...

# E R A S E D...

ROHIT ARORA

tara
India Research Press

**tara**
India Research Press

*An imprint of India Research Press Ltd*

Flat 6, Khan Market, New Delhi - 110003
Ph: 24694610; Fax: 24618637
www.indiaresearchpress.com
contact@indiaresearchpress.com

**2018**

ERASED...

*Rohit Arora*



ISBN 978-81-8386-146-5

9 788183 861465 00299

Printed and bound in India

# *Chapter 1*

He opened his eyes and drew a blank. The sterile white and chrome room seemed unfamiliar. The light falling into his eyes seemed strange – pinpricks piercing his brain, threatening and hostile – as if abnormal.

He closed his eyes hoping to ease his fear. A familiar but numbing darkness took over him, even as he pondered where he was.

Blank!

A cold fear took over him as he recalled what he had seen. A strange, sanitised room that he had never seen before.

*"Who am I? Where am I?"*

Blank!

*"How did I get here?"*

Another blank!

Panic. Wild, uncontrolled, rampant. He tried desperately to calm himself, as he replayed the questions in his mind.

Yet another blank! Nothing! Nada! Zilch!

He sat up in the bed with a jerk. Monitors on the wall began a crazy strobe of lights and numbers. Beeps and blips.

He broke into cold sweat, a familiar blackness enveloping him. He could barely make out the shapes of people rushing towards him, as he passed out…

*He was standing in the same dark hall. He had been in there many times before. It was empty. There was no one there, as always. But he could sense the words… He felt as though he was waiting. As though he had waited too long to be heard.*

*"If I have to be sorry and become someone that I am not for my entire life, I would love for it to be with you," he said to someone who he could never see.*

*"But I can't…." A melodious voice reverberated across the hall.*

*The answer incomplete, interrupted again.*

This time, only to be completed by someone else.

'Dev...' Someone was calling him. 'Hey…Dev...'

He sensed the urgency in the voice, tried to respond to it.

A voice pulled him out of the dark hall into the now bright light of that strange, white room. A face – unfamiliar, yet… He opened his eyes; his fingers felt the warmth of a skin, not his own. A woman in red bent over and asked slowly, 'How are you?'

A wan smile adorned her small white face, her eyes glistening with unshed tears. He kept looking at her for some time. His face took on a puzzled look, as he tried to put a name to the face.

Blank!

*"She obviously knows me. But who is she? Why is she crying? Where am I?"*

It seemed to him that he had already had a long conversation with her in his dreams. That this was right, and yet... Her face took on an expression similar to his – bewildered, yet concerned and afraid.

'I am fine,' he said brusquely.

Seeing her smile fade, seeing the questions in her eyes, he pulled his lips into what he felt might be a reassuring smile.

His eyes closed once again, even before the words could reach his ears.

'I am so...' She stopped.

All she could hear was his breath and some broken words. So unlike him. Gone was that man she knew. The one who had done what he had. The one who had...

This man did not sound like him. But she couldn't help but smile.

The wait was over. He was awake. And that was enough for now.

# *Chapter 2*

## 10 DAYS LATER

'Welcome...'

The woman from the hospital called out to him, opening the door to her flat.

'Nice house,' he said, trying to recall her name.

She had been in and out of his life a lot lately. An unfamiliar familiar face, the one who told him his name. The one who flitted in and out of his room after casually throwing her name into the almost nil conversations with him. The one who was talking to the doctors. The one who wanted to know why he didn't remember anything. The one who tried to tell him that it would all come back, that he needed to take it slow.

'...Nidhi?' he said, hesitatingly.

'It's Neeti,' she smiled.

They walked across the hall to the last room. She switched the lights on and pulled the curtains from the glass window.

It was dark outside; the night had grown thick. He walked to the window and stood beside her. A noisy auto passed down the road dimly illuminated by the old, ineffective street light; the room remained silent, unperturbed by the clamour outside.

'I am in the other room, if you need anything,' she said, putting the TV remote on the bed. 'You won't sleep here?' he turned towards her.

She looked at him with a smile. He had become used to seeing her day and night in the last few days, unaware of who she was, unaware of what they were. The only thing he knew was her startling beauty and selfless care.

'We are not married.'

She walked towards the door without waiting for him to respond. Her small steps halted as she reached the threshold of the room; something was left, perhaps something better left unsaid. She paused, unsure what to say. How much to reveal. She knew he was waiting to hear something, just a little reluctant to ask; perhaps scared to find out something which he wasn't ready for. She turned with a slight lift of her shoulders, as though she had decided that she needed to elaborate.

'I don't want to lie.'

She came back in. It was difficult for her to undo him like that, especially after what he had told her all those months ago.

'I did ask you out once.' Her cheeks didn't turn red, as she told him the first new thing about his past. 'But you said no.'

Dev kept looking at her face for some time, trying to weigh what she had said; no words followed, the eyes didn't convey anything and the face remained smooth, unreadable, devoid of expression. He sat on one corner of the bed silently.

'What's wrong?' Neeti asked. 'I know you have many questions. I just didn't want to answer them in the hospital. But we are here now and I know everything will be fine.'

She sat on the bed beside him, her hand on his knee. Dev turned his head towards her.

'No questions, not yet,' he said, slowly. 'No...there is one, I think,' he paused. 'Every morning when I woke up in there, in that hospital, I…' He took a deep breath. 'I just hoped to see a new face every day, but all that I got was you. You and that doctor, who I don't think I know. When you told me we would go home, I thought I would see my family, finally.'

'You…'

'Don't I have anyone?'

He cut in, eyes closed, trying to hold the tears inside.

'You have me.' She knew it wasn't enough, not to him at least. 'And, you had some really beautiful people around you who loved you a lot,' she paused.

'You were travelling with your parents when this happened – the train accident. They were not as strong as you are.' Her voice didn't falter as she uttered the words she had been holding for nine months, each time wondering whether she would have the joy of hearing him again.

'And...?'

'And what?'

'My wife? Or...' he paused. 'I mean I must have had a really strong reason to say no to such a gorgeous girl.'

'You,' she smiled for the first time since he had entered her home.

'She was. But it's not easy for a girl to wait for someone who might never wake up, ever, and nine months is definitely *too long*.' She pressed his hand gently.

'She is getting married tomorrow. I thought it wouldn't be right to inform her about you. This news would only bring grief, I felt.'

'You did the right thing.'

He tried to stretch his lips into a smile, struggling to push the tears back.

'I think that's enough for the day. You should sleep now. Tomorrow is a new day.'

'A new life...for me.'

'That's not a bad thing,' she weaved her fingers in his hair slowly. 'Trust me. Sometimes people who have gone through what you have don't come out with the ability to do anything – to walk, to talk, to think... Take this like a new birth where no one tells you what to do, what to be, who to see, where to go. Everything new; to learn it, live it...'

A faint smile came to his face. 'Have you been practicing this line for nine months?' He laughed slowly.

'Nah...just ten days.'

She laughed and turned to leave the room. What he did not see was the mysterious smile on her face as she walked away.

# *Chapter 3*

## I WEEK LATER

'Dev,' Neeti called out his name for the third time in ten minutes.

He still didn't come out.

She would have walked into his room had it been any other day in the past, but it was not. She was effectively a stranger to him, and… She shook her thoughts and turned to the present. This was her last day on leave from office, which meant her last day as his nurse, his maid and caretaker.

Neeti had decided to make life comfortable for Dev within those six days. And while any other person would have found it difficult to cope with the menacing silence Dev always wore, she knew she had madc a lot of progress in that one week. Distance can never be measured, neither in terms of how much you travel, nor in terms of the time taken for it. It is sometimes as close as your fingers to your phone, yet it may take months and years for that one call to reach loved ones, and then sometimes it may be as large as across cities and countries, yet you may take just days to see those who matter, and still, it might fall short of expectations.

Neeti knew she had not fallen short. She knew Dev would never fall short in her expectations, even if he never took a single step; he would always be there. At least, Neeti believed that or made herself believe so.

'Dev, dinner is ready,' Neeti shouted again. Dev came out of the room this time and travelled the distance from his room to the kitchen.

'What is it?' He said rubbing his eyes, still asleep.

'*Daal chaawal.*' The reply came in the same unaffected tone.

'Do I cook? I mean, do I know how to cook?'

'Will you make yourself great lunch, if I say yes?' Neeti asked.

'Well...maybe.'

'Will you?' Neeti looked into his eyes, a small smile on her face.

'Yes, I will.'

'Yes, you cook. I have pasted all the nearby takeout restaurants' numbers here,' she said pointing towards the side wall, 'in case you don't feel like cooking.'

Neeti continued to pour the *daal* in the bowl.

'I know you hate to tell me anything about myself, but...'

Dev stopped mid-sentence, frustrated and unsure of what to say. All his questions about himself had gone more or less unanswered in the past week; sometimes Neeti claimed she did not know the answer, at other times because it was not good for his health or because she just didn't want to answer, but all the times had become one time too many without answers for Dev in that one week.

'I just feel that it's not the right time to clutter you with information, Dev.'

'Okay, don't, but can you tell me something about my family or my girlfriend?'

'What do you want to know? I have already told you many things.'

'Not many. You have told me bits and pieces.'

'Dev...' Neeti turned towards him. 'Mr. and Mrs. Sareen, your father and mother, loved you a lot and so did Kriti, your girlfriend. You shared more things about your life with me than you did with your parents in 25 odd years or with your girlfriend in three. Trust me. People who were the most important in your life wouldn't have wanted me to tell you everything so soon. I would love to see you getting out of this shell; all of them would have wanted to as well. This is not the Dev Sareen we knew. The day I feel my Dev, their Dev, the real Dev is back, I will walk up to you and tell you everything that you need to know. Don't strain your mind till then.'

Dev's face was as numb as it had been the last seven days.

Neeti had seen him in many phases of his life, but this was the one that scared her the most; a faint smile when she had first brought him home was all that she had seen on his face apart from pain and sadness.

'What?' Dev faltered. He walked out of the kitchen and reclined on the wall. 'What am I supposed to do till then?'

'Maybe…'

'You don't understand, Neeti. I need to know,' he said, without waiting for her response, 'You don't understand how it feels when the only thing that you can do is to think… think about getting anything...anything that is relevant to your life. I sit numb in my room. I get weird dreams. I can't miss my past; I can't plan for the future. All I do is analyse my day again and again and again or dream sometimes.'

He closed his eyes. '...dream of how my family might react to see me alive but then…I dream without faces. Each time I try not to think of anything, I cry, and, each time I try to think of something, I cry. I don't know what to do.'

He opened his eyes, flooded with tears. 'This is killing me,' he forced the words out.

Neeti walked up to him. Her eyes firm, looking straight through his tears.

'I can't even say that I understand Dev, but yeah…I am trying to. Unfortunately, there is nothing much I can do to help you right now, but I promise you that slowly, I will tell you everything. Give me some time; give yourself some time. You will know whatever I know pretty soon. Maybe you should start getting out; spend some time doing stuff. Maybe find a job, watch TV, just chill. When I feel everything is okay, we will have this conversation again. Though, I hope it's never required. I hope you move on more easily than how I will have to...'

## *Chapter 4*

### 7 DAYS LATER

Neeti barged out of her room after trying to ignore the continuous loud noise for some time. Dev was watching something, rather some things, on TV – a sport definitely, or maybe more than one sport. Rotating commentators every few seconds were sometimes praising Messi for a big goal and scolding Dhoni a few times for the sliding tackle he had been attempting. 'Can you not watch just one?' She walked barefoot to the hall, her legs still wet.

'Which one should I watch?' Dev lifted his head back to see her upside down.

'Football.'

'I knew it. That has to be my choice.'

'No, that's my choice,' Neeti smiled.

'I thought we were over the crazy "what do I like – pizza or burger?" thing last week itself.'

'We were, but it's a little difficult to decide sometimes if you find both things interesting. I mean...if you are confused between black sandals and red sandals, wouldn't it become easier for you to decide if someone tells you most of your dresses are red?'

'Yeah,' Neeti stood straight for a while and replied,

'But wouldn't that discard the possibility of me deciding to wear a black dress completely?'

Dev turned back towards the TV. 'There is no point in arguing with you, is there?' He switched to the cricket match and folded his legs.

'You were a die-hard fan of football.' Neeti sat beside him. 'You supported Man U like anything.'

'Really?' Dev smiled. 'No doubt I was cheering for them like that yesterday. See, that wasn't so hard. Now I can enjoy my football with full concentration.'

Neeti kept staring at his face, even as Messi's dribbling kept him occupied for a while. It was the first time since he had come from the hospital that he had smiled for so long, without inhibitions, without second thoughts, without remorse and most importantly – without fear.

Neeti blinked as she realised what had made him smile; it was the same fear, still present, just gone temporarily; the fear of loving something that he shouldn't because he did not know what he had liked before.

Neeti didn't want any "should not" in his life; she knew what she had to do. Perhaps hated herself for doing this...but she spoke again.

'I was joking. You loved cricket.'

'You do realise that you are once again playing with my sentiments…'

'No, Dev, you are doing that on your own,' Neeti countered.

The smile from her face vanished. Dev fell silent; he could see tears pooling in her eyes for the first time since they had come to her house. He could not understand the reason for them, especially on a day when he seemed so happy. Yet, he felt responsible somehow.

'You are cutting down someone really important to me,' she snapped. 'Again and again. Dev Sareen isn't someone's puppet. I feel bad every time you try to act based on my opinions. So what if I am the only person who knows you well? You should not decide if you would eat on the couch or in your room based on what I tell you; you should not decide to laugh or cry, shout or not, based upon my opinion; you should not watch football just because…' She stopped. Her voice became heavy. Becoming emotional was not on her list of desired reactions. She needed it to stop…

'I am sorry,' Dev said. 'I didn't know. I have been acting out. I didn't realise how difficult it must be for you to see me in this condition.'

'Don't be sorry,' Neeti spoke with her eyes closed. 'Just don't depend on me so much. It's too much responsibility for me, Dev.'

'I understand.' Dev hugged her lightly, though, he was still confused about whether he truly understood or not.

A part of him wanted to know everything. A part of him did not understand the secrecy. As far as he was concerned, he had a right to know and Neeti was holding out.

Perhaps, it was time...

# *CHAPTER 5*

## 5 DAYS LATER

'Oh my God!' Neeti twisted in her bed as the sound of Dev laughing in the hall continued infiltrating her ears. She threw the thin sheet off with a jerk and rolled to the side.

'I am not irritated by your loud, fucking laughter, Dev,' she mumbled, as she stood up and slipped her feet into the thin yellow slippers placed beside her bed.

A smile came onto her face as she turned the doorknob; Dev was watching something on TV. For some reason, Dev was finding it extremely funny.

'Aren't you planning to sleep tonight?' She asked, looking at the watch.

It was well after midnight; almost morning.

'Has anyone told you that you look amazingly cute after waking up?' He said, looking at her messed up hair and half-shut eyes. Her slender body, covered in two loose, purple, cotton clothes.

'All girls do. You haven't seen others,' she said, chewing her lip. 'By the way, I would've been equally happy if you had said this to me in the morning.'

'Sorry to wake you up, but this show is extremely funny. I wasn't able to sleep today. So I thought I would watch something.'

She flopped on the sofa next to him. 'How can you sleep at night, when you sleep the whole day!'

'What else can I do? You don't let me out. You don't tell me anything about my past. The only thing that I can do is to watch something, sleep or think. You have a problem with the last option, so I am left with only two.' She stretched, adjusting herself in the sofa again, her neck rolling back to the armrest, her face towards Dev. 'What do you want to know? I have already told you enough. Haven't I?'

'No, you haven't.' His voice lowered. 'I still don't know who I am.'

'That is something you need to find out.'

'Again?' he snapped. 'That's what I have been hearing whenever I try to talk to you about myself. I know about my parents, my girlfriend, my accident, but what about me? I want to know more about who I was. I want to go out and do things – find a job, meet people, do stuff...'

'And when did I stop you from doing that?' She sat up. 'I think I gave you the idea of going out, finding a job, meeting people and doing stuff a few days back.'

'Yes, but how will I do that if I don't know who I am?'

She took a deep breath. 'I don't want you to mess up your life with stuff from your past. You have a chance to reshape yourself any way you like. Why do you need to know what you did? If you keep worrying about what you were, what you liked to eat, wear, watched…you will never be able to be what you *can* be now.'

Dev moved close to her. 'Fine! Don't tell me. But I think there's nothing wrong in your telling me what my qualifications were, what I used to do, what I am good at… How am I supposed to find a job, if you are so hard on me?'

'I am not being hard on you, Dev. There is a reason why I don't want to tell you...'

'Was I a terrorist? Was I a really bad man?'

'Now you are imagining things. I shouldn't have let you watch that Bourne movie that day. Now you are seeing conspiracies everywhere.' She stood up. 'Come with me.'

Dev followed her to her room. The first time in almost 20 days that he had gone to her room. Not that she had asked him not to, but he hadn't ever found the courage to. But the situation had changed – he wasn't scared anymore; not of her, not of that house, nor of his life. He felt as though he had known her forever, that she was someone really close, someone he could trust...

Her room was much smaller than his. Neat, organised, what he would expect from her. The cupboard was closed, but he was sure that each and every piece of clothing was carefully placed inside. The pillow cover matched the red bedsheet, which in turn matched the color of the beautiful tablecloth adorning her study table, which was placed beside the side wall.

Neeti walked up to the bed, picked up the sheet from the ground and folded it while he kept looking around her room.

'Come here.'

Neeti was in front of her table. Lying on it was a computer which, once again, had a red flower shining on the screen in the background. He pulled a chair beside her and sat silently. A light flowery scent assailed his nostrils, making him realise that he was sitting too close to her. He looked at the small blue, plastic ring that she was wearing in her ear; a thin white chain gracing her neck and the small titanium pendant hanging from it at the vertex of her cleavage.

He didn't even realise that he had crossed the bounds of propriety, as his gaze moved beyond the boundaries of their relationship. His eyes boring deep inside her purple top... registering that she wasn't wearing anything beneath.

'Happy?'

Her voice pulled him out, forcing him to look in her eyes like a thief caught. He turned his head slowly towards the screen.

'This is your profile,' she said, pointing towards the screen. 'Happy now?'

He remained silent for some time, rejoicing at finally finding the first piece of his identity. 'I am sorry,' he said slowly. Why he apologised was not clear to him either.

She smiled. 'Read...'

'I am an MBA,' he beamed. 'I have worked for so many companies!'

'Yeah...' she laughed, looking at him. 'You are a marketing genius. But do you even know what that is?'

'What what is?'

'An MBA or even those companies for that matter. Do you even remember what you did there? Which of them are corporate giants and which of them are some small companies that you helped for free?'

Dev kept staring at the screen; the words on it made little sense to him, but they did tell him something – he was brilliant, *was*.

'I don't know what you got by looking at this, except some joy *I hope*. I am sharing this with you only because you wanted it.'

'Thanks,' Dev turned towards her. 'It gives me a lot to go on. At least, now I know what I am; what I am good at that it... what I want to be, where I can head...'

'No, it doesn't.' Neeti's words remained as incisive as ever, and as if to prove a point, she added, 'By the way, that show you were watching is called *Friends*; on the DVD player that you gifted to me. The episode that had you cracking up just now was also the only episode that you never liked earlier in the entire series. It didn't seem too bad this time, no?'

# *Chapter 6*

## 2WEEKS LATER

Neeti froze as she entered her house. At a first glance, it looked like a tornado had hit it. Her living room looked like a victim of assault…and she knew that the culprit was in her house, in the room next to her's.

She knocked on Dev's door, trying to keep her cool. He opened the door at the first attempt.

'I am sorry,' he shrugged, returning to his bed.

'Please come out?' she seethed, standing at the door.

'Don't want…' he answered, stopping beside his bed without turning around.

'Don't talk, but come out, please?'

Dev turned and walked towards her, quite untouched by what he had done...

Both of them went to the living room sofa. Dev sat, displaced, trying to figure out the next course of action.

Neeti picked up the cushion and magazine lying on the floor, pulled the small table from a corner to the center and slouched on the sofa beside him, her legs on the glass table top.

'Do you really expect me to ask you – what happened, why are you so angry and other such shit,' She didn't mince her words. 'Especially after seeing the same fucking thing happening to my house for the third time this week?'

Dev looked like a baby that had grown up enough to get shouted at by his mom.

'Why the hell can't you, for once, screw up only your own room so that I can relax in mine after coming back from my shitty office?' she screamed.

'I am...' He stuttered. 'Am... am sorry. It will not happen again. I promise.'

'Good,' she smiled, as she hadn't been screaming at him a moment ago. 'Now, let's talk. What happened? Someone screwed with you again in an interview?'

Dev looked at her, bewildered. Her face had transformed into a beautiful smile; raised eyebrows framing serene eyes, which had been wide open with anger seconds ago.

'Were you...'

'I meant every word of what I said,' she warned, adding in a softer tone, 'now, tell me what happened this time? I thought you were better prepared, weren't you?'

'And where is that book you were reading?' she asked, looking around for the book which lay abandoned in one corner - *Marketing Management*, it read.

'I was prepared, but I will never be able to convince people about my abilities...'

'What happened?'

'I answered every question related to marketing concepts. I even told them everything I had read about my work in other companies.'

'So?'

'That bitch was pretty impressed with my resume, but then she asked about my hobbies and interests...'

'Don't tell me, you couldn't answer...'

'I fumbled when she asked me about this nine month break...I had to tell her what had happened.'

'She rejected you because you lost your memory? She wasn't convinced that you knew your job?'

'She rejected me because I don't know myself.' His voice became louder. 'She was convinced that I had forgotten all the skills. What do I need to do to prove myself to those people? The same thing has been happening for so many days now. And it's all because you won't tell me anything that can help me prove myself to them.'

'That's a pretty lame excuse to justify your failure. I do not find such methods very useful. Stop being a loser.'

'That is rich, coming from someone who isn't helping me

getting back on track...'

'Then why the hell aren't you?' she shouted. 'How am I responsible for your fumbling about your interests, hobbies, values – not once, but multiple times?'

'What should I tell them when I don't know? Should I give them random stuff, a lie?'

'Why not, if you feel you can do it?'

'Did I do that earlier?' Dev exclaimed. 'Am I good at lying?'

'What the hell is wrong with you?' Neeti yelled. She jumped up and stood in front of him. 'How does it matter whether you did it or not? The only thing that matters is whether you want to do it now. The choice has to be yours, Dev, not mine. How can you let anyone control your life like this, even me? Why are you so hell bent on doing whatever I tell you about yourself? What if I turn you into some sort of weirdo that used to be your worst nightmare?'

She paused for a breath. 'I don't want to tell you things because I am scared; I am scared of the power you put into my hands the moment you asked me about your nature, your behavior, your goals, your dreams...I am scared of being wrong, of telling you something which might not be true. I knew you pretty well, but I am not sure if I knew the real Dev.'

She kneeled in front of him. 'No one else can know you better than you yourself, Dev. There are a few things which no one could, no one can and no one will ever be able to tell you. Stop asking. It's your life. You are the only one who can decide how you want to live it.'

Dev kept looking at her face, his gaze cold. All the questions in his mind quietened suddenly, but he knew they would resurface; it wasn't easy to stop that inquisitiveness of his mind...

'Okay,' he said. 'You are right, even I know that, but it's difficult sometimes.'

'I know. But then, I also know that you always loved to find out ways, solutions. If someone isn't convinced of your talent, you will find a way to convince him. I am sure of that.'

The room fell silent. Dev looked at the floor, the mess he had created. He had been complaining about the same thing for days now. It was time to go a different route. He turned his eyes towards her; she was still there, sitting, waiting...

'Your confidence in me gives me confidence. That's why I turn to you for answers when I find myself faltering.' He took out a crumbled piece of paper from his pocket. 'I will find a way out. I am sure now.'

He smiled and threw the paper aside, adding to the mess.

Neeti smiled and stood up. She walked a few steps and picked up the paper; it was his CV. She turned back towards him and threw it on the sofa.

'For once I will not complain that you are littering in my house.'

# *CHAPTER 7*

## 10 DAYS LATER

'Dev Sareen.'

A shrill voice called out his name. He turned towards it and got up from his seat.

The last one hour of waiting hadn't been like the never-ending heart pounding that it had been for the previous interviews he had faced in the last few days. He walked with a confident smile towards the lady in the black skirt and white top. No file in his hands, unlike the other candidates who were buried under paper and portfolios.

'That's me.' He gave a swift look to the ID card displaying her name around her neck, 'Miss Arpana.'

'Mrs....' she smiled back. 'Your file?'

'I thought my resume was already inside.'

'It is,' Mrs. Arpana frowned. 'But you could've carried something.'

'That's all. May I go in now?'

'Come this way.'

She led him to a room and knocked on the door. Her expressions told him that he was on his own.

'Please take a seat, Dev.' The interviewer, a slim gentleman in his early 40s, welcomed him with a smile, pointing towards the chair neatly placed opposite to him. He was wearing a badge – 'Prashant Nagar', it read.

'Thank you, sir.'

'Mr. Dev,' he paused, 'Dev Sareen.'

He turned his gaze from the paper on his desk to the lean man it belonged to, a baffled look on his face. 'This interview is going to be really short because I don't have anything about you on me. Is this a print mistake or have you actually submitted a blank page with just your name on it as your resume?' 'It is intentional, sir,' Dev said, smiling, his face alive. 'And, it's not blank. You need to turn the page...'

Nagar turned the page; it did have thousands of letters coming together in hundreds of words, summarising Dev's life in just 10 sentences. He didn't read it and turned his attention back to Dev.

'It doesn't make sense, Mr. Dev. Mistakes like this are not welcomed in the industry you are trying to get in. Words are precious...They follow formats, procedures, methodologies and rules. This information should have been printed on the first page, I believe. Or, is this intentional as well?'

'It is, sir,' Dev took a small breath, 'And it makes perfect sense to me. I couldn't find a better way to tell you about myself and my experience in a crisp manner.'

Even though Nagar's expression didn't change, Dev sensed that he wanted to know more.

'The first page, a blank, that you see is me, at present.' Dev paused, for effect. 'And the information, what little I have mentioned on the other side, belongs to my past, the one that I don't remember, one that might not truly represent my knowledge or experience at present.'

He swallowed his hesitation and continued, 'I am a patient of amnesia. I met with an accident around ten months ago and came out from a coma a month back. It would be inaccurate of me to claim that I am the same person I was before the accident because I don't remember anything. Those companies, those qualifications and those projects which I have mentioned on the back, I can only pretend to know because in reality, I don't.'

Dev stopped as his voice faltered; his heart had started pounding again; his fear of rejection, his lot with fate corroding his confidence.

He took a small breath and spoke again, 'Even I expected the interview to be short. There is no point in wasting your time and mine, if my eligibility for this position, for this company, can be decided with a brief discussion.'

Nagar continued looking at the blank resume with just the name on it. For the first time in his career, the room, which had seen many broken hearts, many shattered dreams and many happy faces, was witnessing its controller, its master, bewildered, clueless. Nagar had no question, no direction; he didn't know if he sympathised with the tragic story of a brilliant mind or was simply amazed at the beauty of the experience that he had undergone in those last few minutes. It didn't matter what he felt; in the end, reasoning had to win over his sentiments, if not over intuition.

'This is the first time that the person sitting in that chair is smiling and I am not,' he turned his head towards Dev. 'What happened with you is tragic, but even more tragic would be to dismiss you because of it.'

Nagar picked up Dev's resume and folded it gently. 'Memory can be a tricky thing, Dev. I don't remember my first steps and my first words, but I am really good at talking and I haven't forgotten how to walk either. You might have forgotten what these random letters under your qualification stand for, you might have forgotten what those companies stand for, but I am sure the learning you got from them is something no one can take away from you.'

Nagar stood up from his seat, the folded resume in his hand pointed at Dev. 'This paper tells me you still have that creativity, that confidence and that will which made you the best. And I want to see the front side of this sheet filled after a year or two with many more achievements.' He kept the resume in the pocket of his coat. 'And I would like you to earn them at our company. I will keep this paper to remind you, whenever required. Welcome aboard.'

'You won't need to, sir.' Dev stood up with a smile.

The interview was really short, the shortest Prashant had ever conducted.

***

Dev pulled his arm back once again, as he was about to press the doorbell. The smile on his face grew larger with every passing second that he spent in front of the closed door of the apartment.

After imagining Neeti's reaction one more time, he decided not to knock on the door. Instead, he took out the second key to the house from his wallet; it was shining even more to him for some reason. He unlocked the door and opened it.

The house was empty; the TV switched off. Cutlery on the kitchen slab told him that Neeti was back, maybe asleep, tired.

He moved towards her room and opened it softly. She was asleep.

'Please, wake up,' he muttered in a soft undertone. So soft that even his own ears couldn't hear his voice.

He walked up to her table and picked the laptop silently. 'I have to respond to a very important mail honey, sorry,' he said, smiled and walked out.

Sitting in the sofa in the hall, he could still feel Neeti talking to him, telling him how he could and would find a way out, how he must be what he is, how he must not rely on what he had been. He went to the folder with his resume, the one which was full of experience but had no value to him anymore, but couldn't find anything.

'Where is it?' he murmured, looking in random folders, in vain.

Dev typed his name in the sidebar and searched for any files pertinent to him. The search immediately retrieved the file with his name on it. He clicked and waited for the processor to open the file which revealed his life to him.

The word file that opened in front of him was not the same that he had looked at a few days back.

It was larger, with more than a 100 pages in it. The cover page had his name as the title, written in capitals, bold and black.

Dev kept looking at the page for a while, unsure whether he wanted to go any further. He went back to the search results; the system was still doing its thing, trying to find the file he was looking for. He checked the address of the file he had opened; it was stored in Neeti's private folders. She didn't want him to see it. That thought made his need to look at it even stronger.

'It has my name on it. It's about me. So what if she tried to hide it, I have the right to see what she is writing about me,' he reasoned.

The first page he read told him that it was a collection of memories; memories that belonged to him, that were once lived by him; it was his life story.

He kept the laptop on the table and walked to Neeti's room; the door was closed. It was quiet. She was still asleep. He came back, sat on the sofa, the laptop back in his arms. He quickly started reading it…

*'What do you mean by you don't know, Dev?' I dragged a chair and sat down, as Sareen Uncle shouted at Dev again. It was third time in the same week that Dev was having a fight at home.*

*Everyone was shocked; Dev was never like that.*

*'That means I don't know.' Dev remained calm, as always.*

*'50,000 rupeess. You spent 50,000 rupees somewhere and you don't even know?' Sareen Uncle looked at Auntie. She was in tears.*

*Dev had become aggressive. His parents had never had any complaints with him till now, but recently, he had become silent – insensitive, in their words.*

*Auntie had told me that he had just one answer for everything, and right she was.*

*'Even if I know, I don't want to tell you,' he replied. 'I don't need to tell you either. I am earning it, I will spend.'*

*'Dev,' his mother said. 'Son, how can you talk like that to your father? We are not stopping you from spending, dear. We just want to know, so that you don't overspend.'*

*'Families don't work like that,' Sareen Uncle cut in. 'You need to make sacrifices. You need to compromise. I have raised you...'*

*'I don't need a family then,' Dev interrupted.*

*His words may have been gentle, but his body, especially his face reflected his anger, his rudeness.*

'That's me?' Dev looked across the room.

The person mentioned on that page didn't sound like himself to him, but Neeti had written his name on that file.

Page by page, scene by scene, memory by memory, he skimmed through half of his past life within an hour. His face pale, his hands refused to go further, disappointment dwelled in his heart. He closed the file and set the computer aside. He now knew why Neeti had been so reluctant to tell him anything about his past.

The first fifty pages on the file were nothing but complaints, incident reports of fights, of arrogance, of ignorance. Either she had kept alive a deep rooted hate towards him to write down those negative memories of his life or he had actually failed to honor anyone's sentiments, anyone's emotions and anyone's expectations of him in his past. He wasn't a murderer, not a criminal, but a man who had committed poor actions against those who loved him the most. He had hurt the feelings of those who had once surrounded him and maybe were snatched away for his arrogance.

Dev shut down the system and kept it back on Neeti's table. He was silent, shocked and also amazed at the love of the person lying in the room next to him in spite of his having done no justice to anyone in his life.

He went to his room and lay on his bed, pondering over what he had just read, thinking about how he had hurt the sentiments of his parents, girlfriend, friends and Neeti.

He kept thinking about his past actions till he fell asleep.

# *Chapter 8*

## 3 DAYS LATER

'How much?' Dev asked the person who approached him with a thick stack of papers.

'150 rupees,' the man said. 'You want a file for it?'

'Yeah.'

The shopkeeper arranged the papers in the file and placed it on the counter.

Dev gave him the money and turned around with the file.

'Hi.'

Prashant Nagar hailed him as he started walking back towards his three-storey office.

'Hi Prashant.' Dev forced a smile on his face.

'We have a pretty decent printer in our office, Dev,' Prashant said, taking out the lighter from his pocket. 'Why are you wasting your money here?'

'I know,' Dev replied. 'But this one is personal and pretty heavy.'

'Hmmm...'

Prashant lit the cigarette and took a deep drag. 'So, second day in office...how are you finding it?'

'The place is nice. I don't know the people yet,' Dev uttered, staring at the cigarette in Prashant's hand.

Prashant smiled, took another drag, and said, 'People may not know you, but I think it's natural, as long as they and you are interested in knowing each other. They are all very nice and easy going.'

'I hope so,' Dev smiled faintly. 'It's just been two days anyway. I'll make friends once I get on a project.'

'Do it before that. Why do you want to wait till then? Make friends, go out...You will enjoy the experience even more when you get on a project, which, by the way, will be sooner than you expect. I am eager to see how you think; the team even more so.'

'Great,' Dev said. 'But it's not easy to go and start talking to people. They all want to know about you, you know, and I...'

'I understand,' Prashant interrupted him. 'We have a party day after tomorrow. We have one at the end of each quarter. I think you joined at a good time. It will be a great way to break the ice.'

'Party!' Dev smiled. 'Nah, I won't come. Not feeling like partying right now.'

'It would be a good opportunity to get to know the people around you and for them to know you. Don't do anything you don't like. Just meet them, make friends, as I said. It will be good for you, trust me.'

Dev didn't say anything. He watched Prashant taking the last drag of his cigarette.

'It's your choice,' said Prashant, throwing down the cigarette butt and crushing it under his foot. 'I can only make suggestions. Give it a thought. The invite will have reached your inbox.' Prashant walked towards his car. 'I am leaving early today. I think we will work only in the next quarter now.' He smiled looking at Dev's surprised face, 'Enjoy till then, bye.'

'You too.'

Dev walked into the building and came out of the lift as it stopped at the second floor. Greenwoods Ltd, read a white transparent plate fixed on the front wall in bold green and blue. Dev walked towards it; the security guard, still not familiar with his face, looked at him curiously. The small green and blue tag hanging from Dev's belt told him that he was an employee of the company.

Dev kept studying the plate for some time which had the image of a small, white bird with a hint of blue towards her tail right above the company's name.

'It's an ocean,' he said to the guard browsing through the

visitors' log. 'This logo…it's an ocean and it appears as if the bird wants to sit on the waves. Or maybe it was sitting on them and is taking flight towards the green woods.'

'Maybe.'

The answer came from another side, a feminine voice. 'Whatever makes sense to you. We laugh at it saying that the stupid bird is trapped and is trying to run away from Greenwoods. She is committing suicide.'

Dev turned towards the woman; a sweet smile shone on red lips on a dusky face, right beneath a long nose surrounded by a pair of wide brown eyes. In the blue *salwar kurta,* the girl, maybe in her early 20s, looked simple, yet mesmerising.

'You people don't like it?' Dev smiled, 'I find it too conspicuous, but it's good.'

'You are new, right? Take your time,' the girl winked at him and walked away.

Dev smiled silently and walked towards his desk. It was empty. He stared at it for a while and then turned towards the exit.

'Why the hell did I return to the desk? I could've gone back with Prashant.'

***

'How was your day?'

Neeti stepped out of the kitchen, her hand covered in a red fluid as Dev opened the door.

'Okay. Nothing special.' Dev threw the bag on the sofa . 'Are you making sauce?'

'No, it's blood,' she answered, matter of fact.

'What!' Dev jumped from the sofa and rushed towards the kitchen. 'Are you serious?'

'Yeah,' she answered. 'And, I am not in the kitchen. I am in my bathroom, but you can come in.'

'Of course, I can.' He stepped inside. 'What happened?'

'Nothing. I was grating beetroot; my hand slipped.'

'Oh...where are the medicines?'

'Why? Come on, be a hero, take this finger and lick all the blood off.'

'What!' Dev yelled with shock and both of them started laughing. 'You are impossible, Neeti.'

'Just strong,' she smiled and walked back to the kitchen. 'So, what happened?'

'Nothing happened. I told you, it was okay.'

'No, it wasn't,' Neeti took the beetroot and started grating again, carefully, 'I can see that the happy man in this house is gone. You have appeared pretty lost for the last two days. Is something wrong?'

'New job...' Dev set her aside and took the grater from her hand. 'It will take time to know the people, I think. Nothing else...'

'You want to go to a party?' Neeti hopped onto the kitchen slab. 'We have an office party day after tomorrow. You can come with me. It would be refreshing for you, I think.'

'End of the quarter party?' Dev's hands stopped.

'Yeah, you people also have it? They didn't invite you?'

'Yes, we do, and yes, I have been invited as well,' he started grating again. 'But I don't plan to go. Not feeling like it.'

'Why? It's a great way to get to know people, right?'

'That's what my boss also said. But somehow...I don't know. I am not excited thinking about it.'

'Sometimes you have to do things for the sake of it, without excitement. I am sure you aren't excited about the grating either but you are doing so.'

'You always come up with sound logic?' Dev set the plate and grater aside. 'I will think about it,' he said, heading towards his room. 'But not now, of course. I have a little work to do.'

'Second day of office and you have work to do at home? Impressive.'

Neeti smiled. Perhaps things would work out after all. Perhaps the worst was over and Dev would finally stop hankering after his past…a past that he had never wanted a part of.

***

Dev settled himself in bed and took out the thick file from his bag. He turned to the first page with his name written on it.

'I know you don't want me to read it, Neeti,' he uttered to himself. 'But I can't repeat the same mistakes that I had at some point in my life. I haven't been given this second chance for no reason. I need to change, to be better; for others, if not for myself.'

He turned to the next page, the first of his old life preserved by his precious and only friend. After reading two lines, he recalled something; skipped through a few pages and started looking for a particular leaf – the page about a party.

'Let's see what I screwed up at the parties…'

*'You are coming,' I told him with an air of finality.*

*It had been two hours that I had been trying to convince him to come to my birthday party. It was hard for me to understand him sometimes, his reasoning; I was trying my best though.*

*'No, Neeti, I am not,' he replied, his voice soft, but face full of aggression, the kind that was becoming a regular feature with him now.*

*'It's my birthday, Dev,' I almost shouted. 'You can throw your tantrums to others, not me. Why can't you come, even your girlfriend is.'*

*'Because I am not my girlfriend, Neeti. I am Dev.' He looked into my eyes. 'And I don't need people who won't take me...and my tantrums.'*

*Everyone wondered how he got that ability to look into the eyes of those who loved him the most and tell them disheartening things in a plain voice, without any hesitation.*

*I wondered for long, till he actually didn't come to the party*

*I had planned just for him.*

Dev kept staring at the page. The words, scrambling his vision, roaming, playing around in his mind, molded into shapes, forming caricatures, in front of his eyes. His thoughts dragged him into a world where he could feel that moment; it was as disappointing as the words themselves.

## *Chapter 9*

## 2 Days Later

'Did you just bathe?' Neeti asked, as she stepped out of her room.

Dev was sitting in front of the TV, his hair wet.

'Well…I thought I should go to the party with you.'

He turned towards her and froze; Neeti was already dressed for the party. A red silk gown draped her, filling out her curves in all the right places, and floated down to her knees, enhancing her glowing skin. The gown was like a beautiful frame around a stunning painting, attempting to justify its existence, but merely protecting something much more elegant, much more precious and worthier - *a chefd'oeuvre*. He blinked and returned his focus to the room, to the ongoing conversation.

'But you are already ready, which means that I am late. And, you look beautiful by the way.'

'Thanks. But you said no that day, so I said yes to one of my friends. You should have told me this morning that you had changed your mind. It won't be nice to cancel on the poor guy now; the party is in an hour. Nitin is relying on me.'

'Oh...'

'I am sorry. You should go to your office party. That's also today, right?'

'Nah...' Dev turned his attention back to the TV. 'I mean yeah, it is today but I don't want to go there. I wouldn't know anyone there.'

'Come on, Dev. That can be fun. Besides how will you know people unless you go and meet them? Who knows, you might find some interesting friends there.' She sat on the table in front of him. 'Or one interesting *friend* to be particular.'

Dev looked at her face, the honest smile. Somewhere inside him he knew he didn't like parties, still he had a reason to say yes; he needed to change, to improve. The choice was simple.

The doorbell saved him.

'That should be Nitin,' Neeti said, rushing to the door.

'Hi.'

A lean man with a French beard and a weird hairstyle smiled at her as she opened the door.

'Hello, mister,' she gestured him in. 'I must say you are punctual.'

'I'm late only for meetings,' he said, walking in.

'Nitin, this is Dev,' Neeti introduced them. 'And Dev, this is my colleague Nitin.'

Dev stood up, his ears filtering every word coming out of her mouth, his eyes surreptitiously observing every step, every movement made by her guest. He raised his hand towards Nitin with a faint smile; Nitin bore a similar expression on his face.

Dev was suddenly beaming with joy, as Nitin turned towards Neeti.

'You are looking amazing,' he said, striving for calm.

'Thank you.'

She looked at Dev, as if wanting to say something. He knew what she wanted to say.

'Don't worry about me. I will go...I think you two should leave now otherwise you will get late unnecessarily.'

'Good.'

She smiled and headed towards the door. Nitin followed.

In a second Dev was alone in the house. Feeling a bit sorry for himself, he switched off the TV and walked purposefully towards his wardrobe.

# CHAPTER 10

Dev stepped out of the rather small party hall, dimly illuminated with neon blue lights placed below the name which read in red – Shades.

It had been an hour since Dev had gone in, seen strange people walking about, laughing, shaking hands, giving high fives to other strange people, some moving to the bar and others gradually slipping to the dance floor, or some simply standing with other strange men and women. He had sat in one corner with a bottle of beer in his hand the whole time, observing how all those strange to him were not so strange to each other.

People would occasionally step up to the sofas beside the wall to drag their friends onto the floor, but none came for him. He couldn't make up his mind whether he wanted someone to come up or not; he didn't know anyone after all. He waited a long time to finally step up, but when he eventually did it was to leave the place.

He walked across the street and sat on the steps of a shop on the opposite side. The world in front of him was different suddenly, paradoxical, as if he had travelled to a different universe, a different time.

People getting out of rickshaws and taxis trying to find their way to their destinations; a smile of gratitude on their faces as opposed to those who helped them. The clamour outside different than the noise he had witnessed inside; yet he felt at peace.

'What are you doing here?' Someone close asked him. He turned towards the person; it was the girl from the office, sitting right beside him.

'Hi. When did you come here? I didn't notice.'

'I didn't create much noise. You seemed pretty lost,' she said.

'Yeah, I was.'

He turned his attention towards the parking lot across them. 'I was noticing how strange life is. This is a party hall. This street is a lively place. People come here because they are happy, or they want to be happy. They drink, dance and carry on.'

'Yeah...though, you don't seem to be that happy here.'

'Leave that. Just look at that parking guy. He is also drunk, but I don't think he is happy and no one seems to care. We are all selfish creatures.' He turned towards the girl. 'Happiness for us means a smile on our faces, that's it.'

'Life is too short. We barely have time to deal with our

issues and are too busy to include others in it as well.' The girl stood up. 'Come on, get up.'

'No...I am fine here.'

'You could have seen drunk guys in the parking lot in front of your own building as well, right? But you are here. Enjoy it. Come on, let's go in.'

Dev took her hand and got up. The girl dragged him back to the party.

Finally, someone had come for him; the feeling amused him enough to make him follow the strange girl.

'Three shots each,' the girl ordered at the bar, as both of them stood with their heads shaking to the heavy beats of the music. 'TEQUILA!' she said, smacking her lips.

'You look different,' Dev said, looking at her black jacket and blue mini skirt.

'Different! Is that a compliment?'

'A compliment, of course,' Dev said; the glasses had been placed on the counter. 'By the way, I am Dev.'

'And I am Bhawna.'

They picked up the glasses, clinked. The liquid burned his throat as he gulped it in one shot. Two more followed, one after another, and the two of them shuffled towards the dance floor.

'Coming in a minute,' Dev shouted over the booming music; it had been an hour since they had been on the dance floor.

Broken words reached Bhawna's ears.

'Where…you going?' she asked, but Dev had already left.

Bhawna followed blindly after him in the hazy dark, eyes hardly open. She struggled with the knob for a few minutes and opened the door with a jolt, stumbling into the hallway. She managed to garner support from the opposite wall and stood, tottering.

'Dev?'

Her voice reverberated in the empty corridor.

'Yeah, I am here. I think I stepped onto a couple there.'

He looked at her blurred face, hands locating and holding onto her shoulders, his fingers barely able to feel the coldness of her smooth skin. The smiles on their faces disappeared, eyes locked into each other's.

Dev took a small step towards her.

'Would you mind holding me before I fall?' Bhawna held his left hand and removed it from her shoulder. It slipped onto her body and found its place at the curve of her waist, right above her hip bone.

He held her at the waist and gripped her tightly against himself. He could feel her sharply exhaled breath against his chest as their bodies touched. He kept looking into her eyes; the hazy vision starting to clear. The shallow sound of her breathing could reach his ears even through the pounding beats of the music behind the closed door; her heated breath warming his throat. Neither of them moved; the corridor as silent as it could be.

'I am sorry, I forgot you don't remember anything. Well... this is called a kiss,' she murmured.

Her face went close to his, her eyes closed. She tilted her head as the pair of pink lips, glowing dimly in the sharp neon light, touched his. Dev closed his eyes and slowly invited her in. Bhawna circled her arms around his neck, as Dev inched her closer. His other hand moved to her breast, as he continued kissing her. Bhawna pushed her tongue inside his mouth, as his palm pressed against her breast, fingers finding their way around it, kneading it gently. Dev's mind failed him as the passionate kiss went on; yet, he felt an annoying concern, a niggling doubt that he couldn't decipher.

He opened his eyes. Bhawna was still lost in the moment; he pulled himself back and held her shoulders. 'What happened?' she asked surprised, trying to pierce the sexual haze.

'Nothing,' he said, with his eyes half closed. He didn't know what had made him stop.

'I...I will join you in a minute. Going to the washroom.'

Dev rushed towards the men's room and thrust open the door.

'Stop,' he murmured, 'don't touch her. You're not going to do anything, not today, not ever.'

'I think I should leave now,' he said, as soon as he opened the washroom door and saw Bhawna was standing outside, waiting for him.

'I luh?'

'It's late.'

Bhawna kept staring at him. She took small steps towards him, even as Dev took a step towards the door.

She stopped at once. 'If you want to go, go...'

'See you tomorrow then.' Dev smiled and walked towards the exit. 'I can drop you off, if you like…'

He stopped at the door once again.

***

Dev rolled down the window, as the taxi raced along the empty road. Bhawna had her head in his lap, asleep. The faint darkness outside broken intermittently by the headlights of passing vehicles and street lamps was soothing his soul. He had something in his mind, but he pulled himself back to the ecstasy of the moment, staring at street lights rushing past. Everything moving fast, though nothing was moving at all, nothing but him.

'It's strange, isn't it?'

'What, sir?' the driver asked.

'Driving. It's just like our life,' Dev said. 'You can control only the car that you are driving and yet, you don't know if someone else will pull you in an accident.'

'Usually, accidents happen because we look at others instead of focusing on our driving, sir.'

'That's also my point.' Dev turned his head towards the window. 'Where are you taking me, by the way?'

'I was going to ask you...' the driver fumbled.

'Nah...you weren't. You were thinking that the guy is drunk, the girl is asleep, it's time to run the meter, weren't you?'

'No...sir, I was...'

'Come on, be frank,' Dev started laughing. 'I won't mind.'

'Well...yeah. Parties are good business, usually. And no one ever asked me before.'

'I know. I know.' Dev leaned back and shut his eyes.

'Just keep driving around for some time.'

# *Chapter 11*

## Next Day

'Good morning, mister,' Neeti said.

She was sitting on the sofa with a bowl in her hands, as Dev strolled towards the fridge.

'How much?'

'I don't remember,' he said extremely slowly, his voice hoarse. 'I think one beer and one peg of whiskey.'

'Not possible.' She walked up to him. 'Have you seen the time? It's 2 o'clock.'

'Followed by five shots of tequila,' he said, taking out the water bottle. 'You didn't let me finish.'

'Cool. So I assume the party was fun?'

' Sort of.'

He walked to the stove to check the utensils.

'I didn't make anything. They are empty.'

'What are you eating then?'

'Cornflakes.' She raised the bowl towards him. 'You want some?'

He took the spoon from the bowl with a smile, his eyes on her face, the smile not fading from his face.

'What?' she asked, walking towards the cupboard. 'I know something is on your mind.'

He paused for a second, gulped down his hysteria along with the flakes in his mouth, and spoke, 'Ever met a complete stranger and felt something for him in the first meeting itself?'

Neeti turned towards him slowly; her lips widened. She kept the bowl on the kitchen counter and bit her lip.

'Let me guess…You kissed someone, didn't you?'

'How the hell did you know?' Dev asked, surprised.

'Because that is exactly what you had said to me when you kissed Kriti the first time,' she laughed. 'After a party, drunk, talked to her and both of you had made out.'

'I did?' Dev blushed; his hand reaching behind his neck. 'Okay...that's interesting.'

'So you did kiss a girl, right? And? What happened after that?'

'What happened the last time?'

'I told you. You made out at her apartment,' she said. 'You told me. Needless to say I almost died of jealousy and all the other hormonal reactions that anyone can think of…'

'Oh...'

Dev looked at his reflection in the shelf glass door. 'But this time the latter didn't happen. I just dropped the girl home and came back.'

'Who is she?' Neeti raised her eyebrows.

'Someone from office.'

'I know that. You wouldn't have dared kiss someone else's girlfriend there...'

'You remember the girl I told you about that day, the one I met in the corridor?'

Neeti nodded. 'I knew that day itself that she liked you. Girls don't come up to random guys and start making fun of the company logo without any reason.'

Dev picked up the cereal bowl. 'And how was your party?'

'Nothing like yours.'

'Why? I thought… You and Nitin?' He paused to look at her face, but she had turned away. He didn't complete the sentence.

'We are not going out, Mr. Intelligent. Don't try to infer too much. We went, partied, danced, had a little bit of vodka and then he dropped me home. That's it.'

'But he likes you.'

'I know, so?'

'He told you?'

'No. But he told you. No? I found out the way you did. Body language says a lot. The way he looks at me. It isn't too difficult to follow. Girls are good at that and I caught him staring at me many times.'

Dev smiled. 'Doesn't it make you uncomfortable? You are with him and...'

'You are talking as though you don't check me out.'

Neeti's candidness surprised him; he froze for a moment. His eyes turned away from her. He could sense her looking at him.

'Ummm...'

Lying was not one of his specialties.

'Don't say anything. I have this weird habit of making people conscious. I notice everything. Every girl does. And no, I don't mind, but don't try that with that new girl because she might not take it lightly unless she is a whore, of course.'

'Huh?'

'I am not saying that I am a whore, but I am used to having you around. You are living with me and I will not change the way I dress because of that. I am not going to change the way I live for every person who stares at me so. I can live with it as long as you can remind yourself that I am a close friend and stop staring at my butt, or my breasts or...'

'Okay, okay...I got the point.' He held up his hands in

surrender and walked out of the kitchen. 'And this conversation is weird enough to stop me from doing any of that ever in the future. But what is the logic of calling her a whore…'

'No logic. I just wanted to. She is hitting on the new boy in the team at the first party itself. And I hadn't abused anyone in a long time, so...forget it. You wouldn't understand.'

'Either girls are crazy or you are,' Dev sighed, as Neeti followed him into the living room. 'Anyway, tell me something else...I actually slept with Kriti in the first meeting itself? I must've been one hell of a desperate man...'

'No, you were not.' Neeti walked to the sofa. 'That's why it came as a shock to everyone. You never went in for "physical intimacy", as you called it, before marriage and Kriti always complained about you being too…'

'Too...what?'

'Lame, I must say,' she finished the sentence. 'That's what I used to say, but I think you were just…why the hell am I telling you all this anyway?'

'See…that's why you have to tell me things about me. I…' His voice lowered to more than a mumble, 'I misread it. I just screwed up, because I misunderstood myself.'

'What?' Neeti said, unable to hear his words. 'Can you be a little loud? Or are you talking to yourself?'

'I was talking to myself.'

Dev went to his room and shut the door. Jumping on the bed, he opened his bag and took out the file once again. The pages were shining in front of his eyes, words laughing at him.

'What the hell am I reading anyway!'

But it did not stop him from reading further.

*'I think Dev is bored of me,' Kriti said to me; her face sad, her voice low. She was scared, maybe disgruntled to the extent that she had to call me to discuss the failure her love life was becoming.*

*'Come on, Kriti. What happened? Dev might be angry, nothing else,' I told her, even though I knew things were worse than that.*

*'He has stopped even touching me, Neeti. I feel dejected. It's been months since we...' She hesitated a little and said, 'since we...I think he likes someone else or maybe he is just bored of seeing the same body again and again.'*

*'Kriti! Don't think like that.' I tried to console her. That was all I could do. 'Dev might have been very rude but...it is not like him, you know.'*

*'Then what is wrong?'*

*'I don't know. Only he knows. He was never very physical. Maybe you are just reading too much into it.'*

*'He wasn't? Then what were those things that he had been doing for more than a year with me? He was different with all of you, Neeti, and he was different with me. Suddenly, he has become like this, like he is trying to...I had noticed that he was behaving indifferently with everyone, but I had thought he wouldn't do that to me. What he is getting by being so...'*

'How incredibly stupid can I be!' His fist tightened and jaw stiffened with irritation. 'Read in advance, Mr. Dev. Next time onwards, read in advance.'

He took his cellphone out. 'I had better drop her a message before it is too late...'

He set the mobile aside after sending the text and shut the file.

# *Chapter 12*

## Next Day

Dev waved at the security guard at the entrance after stepping inside the elevator. It was brightly illuminated with white LEDs fitted in the ceiling; yet he could feel the light outside shrinking in front of his eyes as the two metal doors slid towards each other. The light, ignored for its presence, shone brightly in front of his eyes for a second before the door closed. He didn't move; the heavy metallic chamber stood still, waiting for its prisoner to become the master. Dev kept looking at the doors and the plastic numbers arranged in a panel beside it. A different vibration in the closed air.

He had no idea where his imagination was taking him, but he knew it was liberating; it was something his mind was craving. He brought his palm forward and waved it over the number pad; his hand's shadow hid a few numbers, his palm still waving in the air. His face awestruck.

Darkness, sometimes, is the only way to find light – he closed his eyes for a moment to see what they were looking for, but that moment didn't last long; the glowing light in front of him was back.

The door had opened again.

A girl was standing outside, her startled eyes fixed upon him, his hand still floating in the air beside the number pad. She took a small breath and stepped inside after getting a sheepish smile from Dev along with a sudden retrieval of his arm.

'Hi,' he smiled, as the girl stood beside him.

The door closed again, no change in light, no sound this time.

'Oh sorry...I am so sorry.' The girl leaned forward with a sympathetic smile and pressed 2 with her long purple nail. 'You don't remember how to operate it, do you? And I was laughing at you. I am so sorry.'

'Huh?' Dev's eyes widened.

'See...these buttons here, they are used to operate the lift. I pressed 2, right? That meant I want to go to the second floor.' The lift stopped with a small jerk. 'See...we are at the second floor. Have you not come to office with the lift before?'

She continued blabbering as if to hide her nervousness. 'I also prefer the stairs, but thought I would take the lift today, maybe so that I could help you. It would be difficult if you forgot everything, right? But see…you learnt something today. You stay in this office and you will learn everything in no time. I am Roshni.'

Dev kept staring at her with bewildered eyes. The girl was obviously a colleague and maybe a friend too and who knows what else...

'You are Dev, I know. Welcome to the office.' The girl walked towards the glass door. 'Come.'

She walked in as Dev followed her.

'Good morning.' Bhawna winked at him as he entered the floor.

Dev looked at her, surprised. He hadn't heard from her over the weekend after the party. He hadn't expected much, but a welcome smile and a wink were definitely more than "much".

'Good morning,' he said. 'How are you?'

'Dejected,' she said, leaning over the wall of her cubicle. 'Not every day that someone leaves me in the middle of...'

'Hey...I am sorry, okay. I messaged...'

'Let's talk later,' she intervened. 'Prashant was looking for you. Go see him.'

'Any idea what it is about?'

'I know exactly what he is going to say, but I won't tell you. His cabin is 15 steps from here. You can see him now, if you are that curious.'

'I will do that.'

'Dev! Come in.' Prashant beckoned him inside the cabin with a smile, as he knocked at the semi-transparent glass door.

Dev walked inside and settled himself in a chair without waiting for permission.

'Bhawna said you wanted to see me.'

'Yes, it's time for you to show what you are capable of,' he said.

'I am getting a project?' Dev raised his eyebrow.

'Yes, but not alone, of course. Because it's going to be your first, I thought it better for you to work with a team of old hands.' Prashant walked to the door. 'Come with me.'

Both men walked back to where Bhawna had left him. 'It's not a big project in terms of money, but in terms of learning experience and satisfaction, a person like you would like it a lot.'

'You talk like you have known me for long, Prashant,' Dev smiled.

'I don't take too much time to get a fix on people. I thought the interview was enough for you to get that.'

They stopped beside Bhawna's cubicle; a number of people got up seeing the two of them there.

'Dev, this is the team.' Prashant waved his hand. 'And team, meet Dev. You have already heard his introduction from me during our team meetings, so make him comfortable. He is going to work with you on the NGO project.'

'Bhawna, brief Dev about the project. I need not tell you that he needs encouragement.'

'We are quite eager to see how he thinks, sir,' Bhawna replied, with a beaming face.

Dev's expression didn't change. His eyes looked over the people standing there and stopped at the most familiar face; the one he had been so close to.

'NGO project. You are going to brief me here,' he paused for a second, 'Or we can go to the canteen and discuss it over coffee?'

Bhawna walked towards the door. Dev kept staring at her for a while, then followed.

Dev and Bhawna were sitting at the table with two mugs of coffee. The rooftop restaurant, better known as the canteen among the employees of GreenWoods, was famous more for the roof and the open air seating arrangement outside the kitchen area and much less for anything else, including the food.

'I am sorry for leaving like that that day,' Dev said, taking the first sip from his mug.

'It's not fine, if you were hoping to hear something else. And it will really not be fine unless you tell me where you had gone, leaving me alone in that dingy corridor.'

'I can't tell you,' he sighed. 'It's...complicated. You wouldn't understand. And it's a little embarrassing.'

'As you wish,' she sipped her coffee. 'Then let me brief you about the project. The client is an NGO called Rang De. They are not a typical NGO. I mean they are not into collecting donations and doling out free food, promoting education and taking care of children and all that. They are money distributors of sorts. They raise money from people and give funds to small shop owners, poor people and other forced entrepreneurs like rickshaw drivers, electricians, people into animal husbandry, poultry, sewing etc. so that they can invest it in their ventures.'

'That's good. In a way, they're trying to solve the problem at its root; a long-term solution.'

'That's how they also describe it.'

'How do they make sure that people actually use the money for their businesses and not for their personal gains?'

'They take the money back,' Bhawna smiled, at Dev's quizzical expression.

'They don't hand out money just like that and forget about it. Rang De takes it back from the people they give the funds to in installments, with interest, just like banks, just that the interest rates are low enough not to torment the poor.'

'Nice. I like it. It would be good to develop something for them.'

'Good that you like it because you have a major role to play. All the members of this team – Me, Radha, Sandy, Jaggu – are handling multiple projects simultaneously. So we are actually looking forward to some good ideas from you. We need to make some print ads for them, a series of communication strategies.'

'By when?'

'We have time, but it would be great if you could come up with something by the end of next week,' she paused to take the last sip of her coffee; Dev wasn't even halfway through.

'You can ask any one of us if you have doubts. You start right away. All of us will provide as much assistance as possible, as and when required. If you feel it's too difficult or you are out of ideas or uninterested, you can tell me; the rest of us will take it up on a priority and try to finish the project.'

Bhawna got up.

Dev continued taking small sips. 'Tell me something else. What did you do on Sunday?'

'Dev,' Bhawna said. 'Let's keep it professional.'

'You are still angry?' Dev uttered with surprise. 'I thought we were fine now.'

'Why would I be fine with a guy who insulted me by walking away in the middle of a passionate kiss...' She added, after a brief hesitation to complete. '...for some strange reason.'

'You want to know where I had gone?' he asked, his lips pressed into a thin line.

'I am not going to ask,' she said, continuing to stand in her place.

'I had gone to the washroom, remember,' Dev said, trying to figure out how much to divulge.

Bhawna stared at him for a while and sat down again. 'Don't tell me you masturbated...'

'No...no...' The words jumped out. 'Of course not. How can you even think that?'

'Then what am I to think?'

'I lost control. That's it,' he said, keeping his reservations to himself. 'I threw up. I had a little too much to drink, so I threw up. It spoilt my mood completely. I wasn't feeling too good, so I left.'

'Oh...I get it now. That's a possibility.'

'So everything okay between us?' Dev asked.

'There was never anything between us, except for that small moment maybe, but would you like something to be there?'

'I would, definitely.'

'Then everything is okay.' She smiled.

People came, talked, laughed, but no one caught their attention. Dev discovered that sometimes a few words could change one's perspective; that the words could have an impact stronger than any other force. That the words didn't care for anyone or anything; couldn't be scared, tamed or bothered, given the weight of emotions that they got. That the words overcame feelings of hysteria, especially the kind that he had experienced in the corridor at the pub that night.

It had been hours since they had entered the cafeteria; started that conversation which neither of them could remember. They were too absorbed in each other to think of the office that had brought them together or of the rooftop which had brought them closer.

None could intervene, none except nature.

'I think it's going to rain,' Dev said, interrupting Bhawna who was laughing at some anecdote about her school days.

'OMG! It's already dark,' she laughed. 'The rain doesn't matter. We didn't go back to office, Dev. Prashant will kill us.'

'He will understand,' Dev smiled.

'Shut up,' she said. 'Let's go. It's almost seven. Let's show our faces to someone before we leave.'

'But it's 7:50 already.' Dev showed her the glowing dial of his watch. 'I don't think "someone" will be in the office now.'

Bhawna didn't say anything. Both of them looked at each other and burst out laughing.

'Will I get to drop home the most creative girl of our office?' Dev said getting up.

Bhawna closed her eyes slowly, once. Dev didn't wait for her to say anything; he held her hand and walked.

'It's a beautiful flat,' Dev said, looking at the interiors of her apartment.

She stayed in a 14-storey building just two stops from the office.

Dev had bid goodbye twice, standing outside the beautiful building, hoping to get an invitation for coffee from her.

'I know,' Bhawna replied from inside, she had gone to her room. 'Why don't you check out the balcony; the view is amazing.'

Dev opened the door to the balcony and walked up to the three-feet high railing. He leaned over; the view was mesmerising. He could see the whole city glowing like a marriage hall from her 12th floor apartment. His eyes took in the lights, as his mind took flight. Many thoughts passed by; his mind remained calm, the aroma of rain-soaked earth soothing his senses.

'Isn't it beautiful?' Bhawna's voice floated towards him.

'Yes, very,' he replied, turning towards her.

She had walked the distance to stand beside him. She had changed her clothes; no coffee in her hands. Dev turned to look at her face, to her lips that shone in the light spilling onto the balcony from the apartment.

His hand skimmed over her flat stomach to her waist and he turned her around to hold her firmly. His other hand moved to her neck, slipping into her hair. He pulled her closer and kissed her.

His hand moved from her waist; his fingers could feel the cold metal. He unzipped her dress with a swift downward motion of his arm; his senses tantalised by the texture of her bare skin. His hands slid the dress from her body, releasing her breasts to rest in his cupped hands.

Bhawna took a deep breath. She moaned something.

"Take me inside," was all he could make out of that whisper.

# *Chapter 13*

Dev turned his head to look at the beautiful lady lying next to him. Her smooth, dark skin glowing. He traced his finger along the line of her breast; she slept unperturbed. His eyes moved to the small alarm clock at the bedside. It was 2 o'clock.

He had been awake, staring at the walls and ceiling for more than an hour now, unable to sleep. He held his head looking at the clock and sat up without making a sound. He walked barefoot towards the balcony and opened the door. The cold breeze chilled, sending a shiver across his bare body. He stepped outside and shut the door; his legs were freezing, yet he moved to lean against the cold metal of the black railing.

The world before him was much changed from what it had been when he had noticed it last. It was dark, silent, deep, horrifying, but meaningful and united to him. He closed his eyes and spread his arms open. With one deep breath, his chest went cold as the freezing air rushed in, but he didn't shiver. He had never felt more alive.

He opened his eyes slowly and turned his gaze towards the road; there were people walking, vehicles running, lights glittering. Even though he could not hear anything, he could sense the clamour. He went back inside, picked his mobile and came back out. His fingers quick on the keypad, as he typed the message to Neeti.

'Awake?'

Something brought a smile to his face. He didn't realise how long he had been standing outside, until he was interrupted by his mobile. A message that he had hoped for, if not waited.

'Yeah. Something wrong?'

The reply was from her.

He didn't give a second thought and called immediately.

'Is everything ok, Dev?'

'Yes. Yes and yes...I am at Bhawna's house.'

'I know. That's why I am a little concerned. Everything go fine? You don't seem alright.'

'No, no...Maybe because it's cold outside.'

'She threw you out of her house?'

'Shut up for a second,' Dev laughed. 'I didn't call you in the middle of the night so that you could take cracks like that.'

'So why did you call then?'

'I want to tell you something. 'I wrote a poem…'

'You called me this late to tell me that you wrote a poem?'

Neeti asked; she sounded exasperated to Dev, but in truth there was a smile on her face.

'Yeah...please hear it and don't laugh or say anything, not till I tell you I'm done.'

'Okay, start,' she said.

Dev took a deep breath, clenched his lower jaw to stop the tremor. Neeti remained silent, unperturbed by the long silence. He gulped and started...

'I came out, of the closet closed

hoping the air, is dark and cold

glistening glares, and blinding shines

is the world, beneath my eyes

silence a myth, night a ruin

no depth in the sky, no stars, no moon

closed is this world, in brightness so horrid

back I go, from yet another closet.'

Silence prevailed on the line for some time as Dev uttered the last few words; Neeti was stunned that moment. It was as though the old Dev had returned; the Dev she knew, the one who had felt like the world had closed in on him and that he had to do something about it; the Dev who had landed in a coma all those months ago… the Dev she wanted back, but…

'It's done.' Dev's voice intruded into her thoughts.

Neeti kept quiet even though she knew Dev was waiting for her to say something. Every word that had come out of his mouth dwelled in her mind, kept her busy with her own thoughts.

'Neeti,' Dev whispered again. 'Was it that bad? Did you fall asleep?'

'No, Dev, it's amazing. I don't know what to say. I am happy.'

Dev smiled. 'Did I write poems earlier?'

'It doesn't matter. You do now. And that is all that matters. I had found another one in your pocket the day you came home from the party. I didn't say anything then because I felt you didn't want to tell me.'

'Oh, no, I didn't tell you because I didn't remember that one. I was too drunk. I thought I had lost that.'

'Can I ask you something?' Neeti asked, hesitantly.

'Yeah.'

'What is wrong?' There was obvious concern in her voice.

'Nothing. I am happy. Just lost my virginity again.'

'Good for you,' Neeti laughed, took a deep breath, before continuing. 'I don't need to hear from you to know that you are feeling odd. I know you too well. What's bothering you?'

Dev sighed. 'I had a wonderful day today. But it was strange. Bhawna is a really nice girl. We talked for the entire day, but she was the only one talking at that table. I didn't have anything to say. I don't know how long it is going to last like that.'

'You sure this is the problem?' Neeti asked.

'Yeah,' Dev replied. 'Or maybe no. Maybe she just reminded me again that...that I am blank. Maybe I was jealous to hear all her funny school stories and crazy college tales. I don't know. I am confused.'

'Instead of being jealous of her stories, try to love them. At the end of the day, stories don't matter because no matter how good or funny they might be, they are stories. Look past them and move on in your present. Also, all her stories were a way to get closer to you, today; that is in the present and is the only thing that should matter. If you feel you don't have anything to tell her, she should have been the one to hear this poem, even before I did. Dev, I have never found you short of words, how can she? Don't worry; things will continue for as long as you want them to.'

Dev turned his head towards the sky; tears rolled down from his eyes. Someone was waiting for him inside. He could sense it, even though Bhawna was asleep.

# *Chapter 14*

## 10 DAYS LATER

'Dev,' Bhawna called out from behind, shielding her face with her hand from the scorching mid-day sun. She had been looking for him for long, but no one seemed to know where he was except Roshni.

'He must be busy standing alone on the terrace,' Roshni had said. 'Poor guy, seems to be trying to recall something all the time. He is so lost.'

'Dev!' Bhawna shouted this time.

Dev turned towards her with a startled expression.

'Hi,' he smiled, refusing to react, still bemused. 'When did you come?'

'Long back. What are you doing here? Was looking for

you everywhere, tried to reach you on your cell, but you didn't answer.'

'Sorry.'

He took the phone out from his pocket. *18 missed calls*; he didn't check any and kept the phone back in his pocket. 'I didn't notice. I was...thinking.'

'What? Why do you think so much?' Bhawna stood beside him. 'Half of the office is talking...'

'People noticed?' Dev raised his eyebrows.

'If you stand like a zombie in front of the entrance or try to recall how a lift is operated, people will wonder for sure; hard not to notice.'

'Roshni told you about the lift incident? I am just trying to learn something all the time. I observe people, things, machines and even buttons, maybe. I like to read everything and everyone. And this is a lovely place to do that. Every thought is refreshed, rebooted when the cold air, sneaking in from below, strikes you on your face.'

'I've stood here for quite some time before, but never felt so.'

Bhawna walked up and leaned against the wall. 'I think you just like this place a lot.'

'Maybe.'

Her smile vanished, as she spoke. 'You didn't even notice me and I was looking for you everywhere...'

'Hey...sorry. Don't be mad at me. I am an idiot, you know. I just get a little lost sometimes.'

'Good, I saw you people here,' said Prashant, as Bhawna and Dev walked back to their desks. 'How is the new boy doing, Bhawna?'

'Great, sir. Working on the project.'

'Good. Dev, I see you are gelling with the team. Do a good job. We have our first round of presentations next to next Friday; be ready with something concrete by then.'

'Friday,' Dev uttered. 'That is around two weeks. I will definitely give you something great by then.'

'I know,' Prashant said and left.

Dev looked at Bhawna. Both of them understood that it was time to spend the night alone.

Dev dropped Bhawna at her apartment and returned to his. He slipped the phone back into his pocket after disconnecting the call as the lift stopped at his floor. He had been talking to Bhawna all the way to his building and would've continued talking had he not been concerned that Neeti would scold him for being over-involved. He walked towards the apartment with tired legs only to find the door already open; Nitin was standing outside, smiling at something.

In a moment, Neeti leaned out and both of them kissed. Nitin turned to walk away without even noticing Dev's presence.

'Don't shut it,' Dev said, holding his hand out as Neeti tried to close the door.

'Nice to see you, Mr. Dev. Don't tell me, you've come to pick up your clothes.'

'No, I haven't. I am staying the night,' he said.

'Oh...good to know. Great to have you here, sir,' Neeti mocked. 'We have a lot of catching up to do.'

'I must say that we do,' Dev said, crashing on the sofa.

'First, me.' Neeti sat beside him. 'How is it going? How is she?'

'She is good. Very good. And I am happy with her. We have become very close in just two weeks.'

'Less than that,' Neeti replied. 'And I can see that you two are *really, really* close. Did you write anything else? Did you tell her about your poem?'

'Nah to both questions. We are still in the phase of getting to know each other. I will tell her slowly, but she knows I am into creative stuff. We are working at an advertising company after all. I am sure she loves it, so she will love the fact that I like these things.'

Neeti looked at his face for some time. This was the first time Dev had said something about his likes and dislikes firmly, instead of asking about himself. She stood up, delighted and sat on the table in front of him.

'Good.'

'And how are things between you and Nitin?' Dev asked.

'Good...good and slow.'

'I saw you two kissing.'

'You did?' she blushed. 'He is a sweet guy. It is nice of him to understand what I have with you here. He understands that we are friends, didn't react and was very supportive. He didn't ask many questions either, so I felt he deserved it.'

'That's bad.'

'What?'

'You kissed the poor guy because you felt he deserved it? Not because you actually feel something for him?'

'I don't know. How else am I supposed to start liking him? That's what I look for in a guy – how much he can understand me, how much he cares and how much he trusts me. He is scoring well on all the criteria, so you could say that I kissed him because I am starting to like him, finally. What about Bhawna? Does she know that you stay with me?'

'No.'

'Why? How do you think she will react to the fact that her boyfriend...'

'I don't know. I really don't, but I don't want to freak her out. I don't even know if I am in a real relationship or not. We haven't really had something concrete apart from...Leave it... Where is that thing I had written, the one you were telling me about that day.'

'I have it right here.' She took a piece of paper out of her pocket. 'I was showing it to Nitin. He liked it. I love it.'

'You like every crappy thing I do.'

Dev took the paper from her hand and started reading:

*I saw a man lying in the dwelling of cold night*

*I saw a kid crying in the flickering blue light*

*They say don't drink, it blurs your world*

*I saw a clear sight...Just beside the Shades' bar*

*I heard someone shouting, there was a rickshaw I believe*

*I saw a coat, a vest, a note*

*At my table someone said - Money is what? Spend and enjoy*

*I saw a different fight... Just beside the Shades' bar*

*I saw an old woman with some coins on her sheet*

*I saw the filled one in my hand, the empty at her feet*

*I recalled someone saying - You die once in your life*

*I died many times... Just beside the Shades' bar*

'It's okay...' Dev set the paper aside. 'I have a feeling I can do better.'

'I do too.' Neeti took the paper. 'But it's good. Keep trying. I am sure you will get some lovely ideas. You will write...'

'Ideas...' Dev interrupted, his voice loud and face irritated. 'I am in urgent need of them, the right one that is and I am not able...' he shouted angrily.

'Why? What happened?'

'This project for an NGO for which I am supposed to

make an advertisement, but I am not able to think at all. The presentation is due in fifteen days.'

'You got a few days, right? You will think of something. Don't worry.'

'I hope so. We are going to Bangalore for five days to meet the client. They might take us for a field visit to get a better understanding of their work and what they are expecting.'

'That's great,' Neeti smiled, 'And who are we?'

'Me and Bhawna,' Dev smiled back, taking his phone out again. 'I hope I get something good,' he said, replying to a message; Bhawna had already started missing him.

Dev stood up and walked to his room. He was going to make someone a part of his life; he needed some directions, he needed his bible, his diary.

# *Chapter 15*

## 6 DAYS LATER

Dev looked at the well-maintained, smooth road, which could beat an average city road of most states of the country any day, from the back seat of the car driving them through the village to their destination.

It was not a sunny day, like the previous two, to add even more charm to the sylvan world they had landed in for the field visit. Leaves on both sides of the road flew in the air as the speeding car rushed ahead.

'It doesn't look like a typical village,' Dev said to the man sitting in front.

'If you are comparing it to villages of the north, it doesn't,' the man said. 'But it *is* a village with age-old village problems...'

'Like?'

'Like inadequate facilities – water, electricity, modern technology, employment etc. Even though the houses you see might look pretty well off, they are not. There are kids who don't have schools to attend, and in some cases parents, who don't send their kids to schools because they cannot afford to. There are many more things like that.'

'They don't have internet connectivity either,' Bhawna said, struggling with her Wi-Fi-enabled smart phone, as she gave up on her attempts to open Google.

Dev smiled and turned his attention back to the window. They had seen a number of places in the last two days and met a few people. The organisation had divided their stakeholders into different categories – those who sought money, those who lent and their own employees and others, who came voluntarily to help for the cause; Dev had met them all, Bhawna a few.

The vehicle stopped beside the road after a few minutes. Dev could see small houses nearby.

A young man came close to the car; he was wearing a tag which told Dev that he was a volunteer.

'Hello, sir.' The man in his early 20s raised his hand towards Dev, as he stepped out of the car. 'I am Kiran. I help Rang De conduct field visits during the weekends or other off days.'

'Hello, Kiran.' Dev shook the hand. 'I am Dev and this is Bhawna. We are both from GreenWoods. You must be aware that we are not here for any investment related visit. We are working on a project for Rang De, chalking out a communications strategy for this organisation.'

'Yes, sir. Swarup sir informed me. Rang De is doing a great job. I have always felt that the same is not highlighted correctly. We deserve more credit from people than we are getting right now.'

'We will make sure that you do,' Dev replied, while Bhawna stood silent beside him.

Kiran took the lead as all of them walked towards one of the houses down the road.

'What happened?' Dev murmured into Bhawna's ear as she came closer. 'You don't look happy.'

'What is there to be happy?' Bhawna replied, irritated. 'We are doing such a big project for free and they couldn't send someone who is their own employee, forget some senior person.'

'It's an NGO, Bhawna,' Dev muttered. 'I think it's best for us to roam with a volunteer to understand their core values and functioning. We couldn't have experienced it better with anyone else.'

'Leave it,' Bhawna said, trying to get some life on her phone.

Bhawna seemed a little uninterested to him on the trip. She remained silent at Dev's response, silent throughout the trip.

They visited the farmer, weaver woman and a man from the poultry farm; all of them impacted by the money they had received from Rang De or one of its sister organisations around a year back and on the verge of repaying the debt.

Of all the people they had met during their trips, only a few required another loan due to failure in reaping benefits from the first one. Most of the people wanted more money to grow, while the rest were content with whatever they had built, businesses, but most importantly – a livelihood.

The trip ended after two more days; a couple of meetings which, to Dev, more or less meant that the NGO's expectations from the creative geniuses of GreenWoods were high enough to make him conscious of his inability to conceive any idea good enough to present to them.

Five more days had passed and he had nothing but passion for the project. Lost in his thoughts about what he had experienced with those volunteers in Bangalore, he realised there was someone else who needed his attention, someone sitting very close to him in that flight which had taken off for Mumbai an hour back.

He turned towards Bhawna, who was sitting silently beside him, like a beautiful lady aware of her co-passenger's eyes on her face, yet refusing to acknowledge said person. It was as though she was pouting.

'Bhawna,' he said, breaking the silence between the two of them for more or less two days. 'What's wrong?'

'Nothing.'

'Bhawna,' he said again, leaning closer this time. 'Why are you so mad at me?'

'I am not mad at you. Why would I be?'

Dev didn't speak for a moment, took a deep breath and

spoke again, 'I am sorry for that day, but I didn't mean to hurt you.'

'What are you talking about?'

'That's what even I am not able to understand. I...I just wanted to be at that place and I thought your mind was not in it, so I snapped. Sorry,' he sighed. 'This project is very important to me. This is my first and I want to put my best in it. I felt that you were a little uninterested and that just put me off...'

'You know what the biggest problem is, Dev? You wanted to "be at that place" while I wanted to be at that place *with you*. The only reason I had agreed to come to Bangalore was because only the two of us were going to come and I thought we would spend some time together. I thought it would help us get closer, emotionally, but maybe physicality is all you are looking for in this relationship.'

Dev held her hand gently. 'I am sorry. I never knew you were thinking like that. I want to be close to you as well. I love being with you. It's so stupid of me to think you don't want this project, while you were disappointed because you felt ignored. I am happy that you want us to be closer. I want that too and we will be. As soon as this plane lands in Mumbai, you will see another Dev, the one who is interested in everything you like.'

There was no place for disappointment for people around Dev in this new life. He closed his eyes and dreamt of the same fields of that village on the same road surrounded by fallen leaves; this time he wasn't alone.

# *Chapter 16*

## 5 DAYS LATER

*"Hello?" Dev called out again*

*The jungle was quiet. There was no reply except for the dark and ominous silence. He kept walking on the muddy trail, leaving footprints behind him. He was tired, scared and thirsty. He had been walking for what seemed like hours. He looked around, perhaps seeking someone, but there was nothing there, not even the breeze.*

*"I don't want to die here," he shouted and started to run blindly, pulling at small branches in his path, jumping over dark voids beneath his footsteps. He stopped beside a tree, seeing someone sitting at a distance; a man sitting alone near a river with no water...*

*He started walking towards the man sitting on a stone, facing the dry river looking at the other side. Dev walked up to him and tried to see what had caught his attention; he found nothing.*

*"Can you tell me the way out?" he asked, placing his right hand on the person's shoulder. A strange feeling shook him from inside; he felt as if he heard his own question.*

*The man turned towards him; he had no face.*

*"No," he answered.*

'Oh my God!' Dev jerked open his eyes. His breathing was heavy; his chest heaving. It took a moment for his eyes, still startled by the darkness, to adjust to the dim light falling in the room from outside.

'Dev? What happened?' Bhawna leaned over him to switch on the lamp beside the bed.

'Nothing,' he whispered. 'Just a bad dream.'

'Oh...can I get you some water?'

'No,' he said, throwing off the sheet. 'I will help myself. Go back to sleep.'

Dev walked to the kitchen and took out a water bottle from the refrigerator. It had been five days since they had returned from Bangalore.

Dev had finally started working on an idea, but his relationship with Bhawna required immediate attention. He had spent the last five days with her – talking, hanging out, romancing and trying to get closer; it seemed to be working.

Bhawna showed her appreciation by jotting down a

number of ideas, working on a few and even strategising to convert at least one into a presentable advertisement.

Dev opened the bottle with a twist and almost poured the water on himself, as he felt a presence behind him.

'You okay?'

'Yes. Weren't you sleeping?'

' I can sleep later. I don't like to see you stressed,' she said, walking up to him.

'I will be fine,' Dev replied, looking into her eyes.

'Something I can do?' Bhawna looked into his eyes.

'Nah, go, sleep.'

She kissed him gently and put his hand on her waist. She stepped closer and started kissing his neck, slowly tracing a path towards his chest, her hand moving all over his body.

Dev kept staring at the mirrored doors of small closets, his mind removed from the response Bhawna was trying to draw from him; he was lost somewhere deep enough to make him forget about his lover, ignore her desires. He stood still.

'Bhawna.' He held her shoulders. 'Not now.'

Bhawna kept staring at him, baffled. He pushed away from her, walked to the bathroom and shut the door behind him.

Bhawna looked at the closed door for a while and walked to her bed, her thoughts full of anger.

This was the second time Dev had abandoned her. This

was the second time he had left her raging with desire and walked away…

Life always comes a vicious circle. Dev felt like he had just come full circle a few moments back. He didn't know what it meant, but something had happened; something that he could still feel, but make no sense of.

'Awake?' Dev sent an SMS to Neeti.

'What happened?' Came the instant reply.

Dev kept staring at the screen of his mobile for some time; his thumb moving to the speed dial button hesitantly. He looked around; a fat drop of water plopped into the wash basin once again; the sound exploding in his ears. He took a deep breath; he did not want Bhawna to overhear him.

'Saw a nightmare. Not able to sleep.' Another message.

'Should I call? Something's bothering you?'

'Bhawna is sleeping. I am in the bathroom,' he replied to her message.

Another few seconds and Neeti called. Dev's mobile kept vibrating in his hands. Dev took two deep breaths and picked up.

'Hello,' he murmured; his voice barely audible to Neeti.

Neeti was laughing on the other side. It brought a faint smile to his face, as he realised the absurdity of the situation – a grown man trapped in the bathroom trying to talk to another woman while his girlfriend was in the adjoining room. He smiled at the thought and disconnected.

The phone rang again. He answered.

'Okay, I won't laugh now. But what did you expect after reading that message.'

'Shut up. I am really tense,' Dev muttered.

'What happened? Why the tension?'

'I am just not feeling good. Something is wrong.'

'Is it Bhawna related? Or because of the presentation later today? Or is it a bit of both?'

'Both, I think,' Dev replied, suddenly relieved. 'You are amazing, Neeti. How the hell did you know?'

'I know you and I have my ways. Now, care to tell me what's wrong?'

'I am not happy with the Rang De presentation. And unfortunately, I don't have any right to complain about it because I haven't contributed to it.' He walked up to the door, turned the knob and opened it a bit. He could not see Bhawna. He shut the door again.

'It was supposed to be my project, my fucking project, and here I am...complaining about it, hiding in the bathroom. I... I...'

'You are pissed off with Bhawna, aren't you?' Neeti prompted.

'No...not really. She is a wonderful person. The presentation wouldn't even be done to this level had she not been there.' Dev defended her, even as he wondered why he was sharing this with Neeti instead of Bhawna.

'Don't lie, Dev. You are annoyed and you feel this way because of her. You blame her for not letting you finish your work on time. You think whatever she has done is way below your standard; you feel disgusted. It makes you hate her. Accept it.'

'Okay, okay...maybe, I do. Maybe I am irritated because of her, but that doesn't mean I hate her. Now tell me what I should do.'

'Dump her. And change the entire presentation.'

'What? Have you gone mad?' he whispered.

He could sense Neeti smiling at the other end.

'Not really. I have wanted to tell this to you for some days now. But then I thought I should let you enjoy your life. That maybe this is how you wanted things to be…'

'Any other suggestions? It is midnight, just a few hours before an extremely important presentation. This is not the best time to argue about what you just said, so...'

Neeti interrupted, 'Change the presentation without dumping her.'

'That makes more sense, but I am still not able to get any idea that does justice to what I have seen. It's been days. How will I get something good, better than Bhawna's ideas, now? At such short notice? I have been trying to think. I have devoted hours without eating or doing anything just to think about this project, waiting for anything to occur to me, but it has all been a waste, a cliché. I don't know if I am like this or whether I am expecting too much out of myself, but I want something different, out of the box, not like every other tried and tested idea. I...'

'Have you discovered your box, Dev?' Neeti interrupted.

'What?'

'Before trying to find something out of the box, you have to find your box, Dev?'

Dev didn't respond, baffled.

Neeti had an answer that made sense to him, yet again; he just knew it.

Dev continued to remain silent, perhaps because she knew him better that anyone else.

'Our thoughts, our imagination all are restricted to our knowledge of the past, our understanding of the present and expectations of the future, Dev. How can anyone even think beyond this?' Neeti continued, 'To see the world outside this, you have to first trap yourself in it.'

'Still not getting anything,' he said, even though her words were seeping in, making him feel as if he was on the edge of something profound.

'Force your thoughts to think about the project, Dev. They will roam around the same things that you already know, mundane thoughts, clichés. Close yourself in that box first so that you can forget about everything; become blind, but not to your thoughts, only then will you be free to imagine the project from the outside.'

'I want to. But I don't know how.'

'Have you never experienced complete numbness? Have you never started doubting the significance of something, as if you don't know everything yet? Only when you stop acknowledging the presence of colours around you can you actually think of the possibility of a colourless world, of things your eyes are not able to see...'

'I know what you are talking about.'

'Good. Now go to that place and try to think about this project. When you are able to see a new colour, you will know.'

'Yeah, I will and I will call you after that.' Dev disconnected without waiting to hear her reply, opened the door and stepped out noiselessly.

The lights were off. He looked at Bhawna motionless on the bed, her eyes shut. He went to the other room, could feel the silence around him, inside his mind; this day was going to bring new things to him.

# *Chapter 17*

The security guard on the floor opened his eyes gradually. The hazy, half lit sight that greeted him told him that the floor was exactly how it had been before he had fallen asleep – silent, undisturbed and tedious.

He got up from his chair and walked into the lift lobby. He knew there was nothing there, but the niggling feeling that he had heard something was inevitably strong. He dragged his sleep-deprived body to the lift and pressed the button; it opened with a small swish. The elevator was at that floor.

The guard screamed at the top of his lungs as the doors slid open, jumped out of fear and almost fell to the ground: A man was sitting inside on the floor, legs folded, eyes closed. His face was to the back of the elevator; the guard could see only his back.

The man remained calm through the commotion of the guard shouting and recovering from the agonising scare.

The guard took small steps towards the man sitting inside and raised the thick staff to stop the doors from closing once again.

'Hello? Hello, sir. What are you doing here?'

The man, sitting straight, didn't respond. The guard took a few small steps up and was right outside the lift.

'Oye...I am asking you.'

'Do not disturb me.' The man looked up. His voice was harsh, the words forceful, intimidating enough to make the guard step back and hurry to his seat.

The doors of the lift closed once again.

The guard kept staring at the lift for a few seconds and then picked up the receiver of his intercom.

It had been three hours since Dev had been sitting inside the lift, following his conversation with Neeti.

Every guard in the building now knew that an employee from Greenwoods was sitting in the lift like a mad man. It was just a matter of minutes before the entire building would get to know the same; people were coming into office, a new day had begun, but in the quiet of the lift, for Dev, it was still night.

Dev was enjoying every moment of exploration inside his box. Only he knew how deep he had gone in to find what he was looking for. A smile surfaced on his face, as he realised what had been missing. He had found the lost link; viewed that new colour.

Dev removed his bag from his shoulder and took out the laptop. His fingers raced across the keyboard, unaware of the clamour outside till someone pressed the button once again and the doors slid open.

'Good morning, sir.' Dev stood up, looking at the gentleman staring at him. 'I am going up as well.'

Dev smiled and closed his laptop.

Bhawna flung open the door to the office and walked in. It had been two hours that she was trying to reach Dev. Her eyes inspected the floor; Dev wasn't there.

Irritated, she asked the girl sitting on the adjacent desk, 'Has Dev not come to office yet?'

'I think he never left the office yesterday,' the girl responded. 'Someone was telling me that he scared the hell out of the guard early this morning. It's his presentation today, right?'

Bhawna raised her eyebrow. 'Yes, it's going to start in ten minutes.'

She walked towards the meeting rooms, swiftly opened the door to Presentation Room 1 and peeped inside. Dev was already there, so were most of the others involved.

She walked in with a beaming smile, went up to Dev and whispered in his ear, 'I have made some changes in the presentation. Where have you been? I have been trying your cell for ages. This is not done, Dev. I have been working on your presentation since early morning and you switched off your mobile and went to some place without even telling me.'

'I have already loaded the presentation, Bhawna...'

'Didn't you hear what I said? I have made some changes in that and what the fuck is this about you scaring the guard today?'

'That's what I am trying to tell you.' Dev tried to remain calm; smiles plastered on both faces, as everyone looked at them. 'I came to the office early in the morning, got a great idea and made changes in the presentation.'

'You changed the entire presentation?' Bhawna's jaw clenched, as she struggled to maintain her cool.

'Almost,' Dev whispered. 'Just stop worrying. Prashant is here.'

'Hello Dev.' Prashant walked up to them with a short dark man beside him. 'Mr. Sankaran, this is Dev and this is Bhawna. These two energetic youngsters are the most creative minds of my company.'

Sankaran shook hands with both of them and followed Prashant to their seats.

'Start the presentation, Dev.' Prashant turned towards Bhawna, seated in the row behind him, with a confident look, but she was staring resolutely at the screen, her eyes fuming, her lips tightly closed.

'Good morning everyone,' Dev began. 'Everyone sitting in this room has a fair idea about what Rang De is into and what their expectations from us are. So without devoting much time to that, I will try my best to keep this presentation to the point and brief, yet elaborate in context.

The first slide appeared on the big white screen hanging behind him on the wall.

Bhawna's eyes were glued to it. Dev had removed the introduction. He was definitely going to turn this into the shortest presentation ever delivered in that office; something that no one had dared before. Everyone waited for Dev to press the key as the first slide was a blank on the screen, with no heading and no text.

Dev moved to the whiteboard instead and started talking. 'Before moving ahead, I would like to bring something to your notice first.'

He took the marker out from his pocket and started writing, but it didn't work. Prashant clutched his head and turned his gaze towards Bhawna; displeasure obvious on both faces.

'Sorry for the interruption, but is someone carrying a marker in here?'

A young boy raised his hand with a pen.

'Can I borrow it for some time?' Dev walked to the man.

Dev walked back to the board with the pen. "Life", he wrote on the board and turned his attention to the people in the room waiting, if not eagerly, for something to follow.

'Before I begin this presentation, I would like to tell you all a story.'

He walked the entire length of the room and looked into the gathering. Everyone straightened under his gaze, feeling conscious. He looked into every single person's eye without actually noticing a single one.

'When I was a kid,' Dev continued after a brief pause, 'I used to go to school on a cycle. Unfortunately, my parents didn't give me pocket money – only Rs 5, in case my cycle got punctured. But being a kid, I always wanted to have fun, so I came up with a way to manage that sum. I used to eat ice cream with that money, and if someday, I actually had a puncture, I would make a sad little face and convince the cycle guy that he should fix it for free because I would pay the money later. Appearing innocent has its own advantages. The same logic worked with the ice cream guy and the *kirana* store uncle as well. I didn't realise then that what I was doing was actually developing something – a habit, maybe. When I grew up and went to college, all of us friends would to go to a night canteen and though, it might sound cheap, we never had enough money to pay for our cigarettes and food.'

Prashant smiled faintly as Dev spoke. He knew that Dev was leading up to something. He knew that Dev didn't remember a single college day of his life, but he was making up a pretty image.

'At the canteen, we always used to ask that poor old man for a favour and give him all the money at the end of the semester usually. The same story continued during my MBA and then today. Just a few days back, I realised I needed a new mobile phone because my battery drained out on the way home almost every day. Luckily for me, I asked a gentleman if I could make one phone call from his cell and call my cab. But then I decided to buy this phone.' He took out the cellphone from his pocket, brandishing it. 'It cost around 15K and I must thank the inventor of debit cards, otherwise I wouldn't have been able to buy it.'

He stepped forward and threw the pen at its owner. 'But it was yesterday that I realised that what I did is not a habit; it's my lifestyle. It is everyone's lifestyle.'

Dev pressed a key on his laptop. A list appeared on the screen; a list of things he had just described. 'There is one thing common between that ice cream, that puncture, that night canteen and that mobile phone that I purchased. I borrowed something for them all.'

He paused for effect and continued, 'And if I am not wrong, most of you would agree that being a middle class or upper middle class Indian, you too live like this. You borrow something or the other in a day from someone without even realising it. Sometimes we borrow from the vegetable vendor, sometimes from the credit card company, sometimes from friends and sometimes even from strangers. Maybe I am wrong. Maybe there is nothing Indian about it, but then it is because we trust people around us and have been for centuries.'

Dev pressed another key. The slide changed and an image appeared on the screen this time; an image of an old man sitting in front of a small retail store. 'It is this feeling of trust that we have to entice in people once again.'

He pressed the next key hard.

A message, written in blue ink, slid onto the image.

*"Jab aap chhote the maine aapko udhaar diya. Kya ab aap mujhe denge?"*

Dev translated, 'When you were young, I lent to you. Will you let me do the same now? We have to remind people with taglines like – "I don't want donation. I just want to borrow", or "We have no credit cards" – that it's their turn to return the favour that some of these people have done them at some point in their lives. Our print ads should convey this message to college grads, to working people, to everyone who has borrowed money or something from someone at some point in his life.' A small smile grew on Dev's face. 'And I believe we won't leave anybody untouched by doing that.'

The "thank you" slide turned up on the screen, as Dev closed his presentation.

Prashant turned towards Sankaran; he too was smiling.

'I don't think anyone will be able to say no, if you say it like this,' he said; the smile grew broader.

Prashant raised his eyebrow in appreciation with a beaming face looking towards Dev, as they stood up and walked towards the door to discuss future course of action.

'Good job.' Voices rained over him as people started to leave their seats. Every single person of the ten-odd people sitting in that hall came up to him to give a small pat on his back. He accepted each one with a smile of his own.

'Good job, Dev.' Just one voice, clear even among the noise of the crowd, came from a distance. It was Bhawna, standing just beside the door, about to leave.

'Thanks,' he said and smiled. 'I told you not to...'

Bhawna had left the room before he could even complete the sentence.

'...worry,' he murmured the last word with a shocked face.

The door had closed behind her.

# *Chapter 18*

*What happened, Bhawy? Reply at least.* Another message joined the long thread of messages sent by Dev.

He waited for the delivery to be confirmed and kept the mobile back in his pocket. He had left the office three hours after the Rang De meeting and Bhawna had gone missing. Roshni had told him that she had left early, that she wasn't feeling well.

Lips turned in a grimace, Dev stepped out of the office. The guard smiled at him as he reached the lift.

'How are you, sir? Going back to the lift again?'

Dev didn't respond. He took out his phone and unlocked the screen. He had checked the cell around twelve times in last twenty minutes. No message, no call.

Dev was standing in front of Bhawna's apartment. He rang the bell for the fourth time and finally heard some footsteps close to the door inside.

Bhawna didn't shout the usual – who is it? She knew it was Dev at the door. She knew he would come and wait for her to answer.

'Thank God, you opened the door,' Dev said.

The tension in his eyes, his face as calm as it had been during the presentation, but his heart pounding.

'I knew you wouldn't leave,' Bhawna replied curtly and walked in, leaving the door open.

'You didn't reply to my messages.' He closed the door and walked after her. 'I was concerned.'

'That was to make you feel what I felt like this morning,' she said without looking at him. 'How did everything go? I think everyone is pretty impressed with *your* presentation.'

'Our presentation, Bhawna.'

Dev came close and slid his arms around her, holding her from the back.

'Should I take my clothes off?' Her voice dead.

'Bhawna.' Dev turned her to face him.

She was looking in him but there was no love in her gaze, no anger, no pride; she wasn't there.

'What happened? Why are you so angry. I am sorry. You were asleep and so I...'

'Till last night you were in bed with me, Sareen. And you seemed pretty happy about it. What happened in the morning?'

Dev was silent, unsure of how to reply.

'You made that presentation with me and you had no problem. What happened in the morning, Dev?'

'Bhawna...'

'I was awake when you locked yourself in there, but you didn't talk to me. The next thing I know, you were gone. Your cell was off.'

Bhawna closed her eyes for a few seconds as if gathering strength, her breath becoming heavier with each sentence. Dev knew something big was coming; he was about to lose her.

'Bhawna...'

'What the hell do you think of me? I am not your bitch, whom you can abandon in the night, half-naked, without taking responsibility.'

'You were asleep. I am sorry,' Dev uttered. 'I wanted to think and thought it wouldn't be right to wake you up, so...'

'Think? How come you couldn't do that all this time, Dev, while I was slogging away at your work? And why the hell did you think it over again when you had given your nod to my idea *again and again*?'

'I had told you.' Dev tried to remain calm. 'I had told you that I felt something better should come up. I had told you that I wasn't happy. You said that the ideas would be good enough for the client, but...but I wasn't happy because I hadn't given any of those ideas. I wanted to...'

'Great!' Bhawna sighed. 'So now it's my fault that I kept you busy fucking me all the time and I didn't hear what you were really saying.'

'Please don't talk like that, Bhawna. You know that you are important to me.'

'Am I? Really? That's why you didn't even bother to tell me about any of those changes or about your secret visit to the office, and that's why I am getting all the blame for working on your fucking project and leaving all my assignments due. And who would have been responsible for it, had your little trick been a failure today? What would anyone have said on knowing that the lead of this project didn't even know what was going to be in the presentation? Did you ever think of that?'

'No.' Dev turned his face away. 'And...I know you did me a favour and I loved that. It's just that I wanted to do something on my own. I don't know...I was feeling uneasy. I called Neeti and she told me it would be better if...'

'You were talking to *her* inside my bathroom?' Bhawna bit her lip. 'So who else did you complain to about me?'

'No one...' Dev held her shoulders. 'I wasn't complaining about you to anyone. She just told me that maybe I should take the lead and it might make me feel good, and it did. It did, Bhawna. I realised that it wouldn't have mattered to me had those people laughed at me, made fun of me instead of giving me all those compliments. The biggest thing that mattered to me was my pride, that it was my idea. I still feel that the old presentation was amazing and it might have received more appreciation but...'

'But it was mine,' Bhawna said quietly.

A menacing silence prevailed for some time. She took a small breath and said, 'Maybe you should get rid of whatever is mine, Dev, including me.'

'No...Bhawna.'

'Listen, there is no point in us being together if you feel that I outstrip you.'

'Bhawna...you are taking me wrong.'

'No, Dev. Finally, I am taking you right. Go.' She closed her eyes. 'Leave right now.'

A tear escaped her eye. Dev stood there silently, but he knew that he had lost.

# *Chapter 19*

Neeti walked quickly towards her apartment as the lift stopped at her floor. Her skinny legs moved in a crisscross manner to stop in front of the corridor.

'Dev!' Her voice reverberated across the corridor, as she saw a body squeezed within its folded arms, sitting beside her apartment's door. 'Dev?'

Neeti held him by his shoulders. 'What happened?'

She quickly opened the door and pulled him inside. Dev didn't respond.

'Sit.'

Neeti pushed Dev gently on the sofa and rushed to the kitchen for water. 'Did she dump you?'

Dev turned his head towards her. His eyes, half closed; once again, Neeti had read what he had tried to hide.

'She dumped you because you told me about the new idea, but not her.'

'I didn't tell her that you knew about the presentation,' Dev sighed.

'Otherwise she would've dumped you twice?' Neeti threw the bottle to him and sat on the table in front of him. 'The presentation rocked, right?'

'Everyone loved it. It sold pretty well, I think.'

Dev kept the water bottle on the table, unopened; his voice low, sad.

'She will be back,' Neeti consoled. 'Don't worry, she is trying to make you feel her importance. And she might be a little jealous, nothing else. You hurt her ego.'

'What I did was wrong. I actually left her without informing her. I changed the entire presentation. I didn't even think of the effort she had put in. I was mean.'

'You were professional,' Neeti insisted. 'Like her, your ego was hurt because you had contributed nothing to something that was actually supposed to be your baby. If you felt uncomfortable taking credit for something that was not yours, there was nothing wrong in it. It is called work ethic, Dev, and it's sweet of you to have it at a time when most people forget it.'

'She was trying to help.' Dev vented. 'I wouldn't have had anything, had she not been supportive.'

'She is a bitch to have put you in that situation in the first place. I didn't want to say anything, but you are losing sight of the big picture. It's not your fault that she was taking all your time for her pleasure. She had no choice but to help you and has absolutely no right to make it seem as if she did you a big favour. It was the least she could do after all that you...'

'You just don't like her. I know what she has done for me. And a relationship is not about thinking about yourself all the time, Neeti. It's about...'

Neeti held up her hand, as she took her cell out from the pocket.

Dev rested his head between his palm, as Neeti talked to Nitin. Dev could hear his voice even across the distance. His thoughts moved from Bhawna, his ears searching for the unclear words; something was wrong. Nitin was shouting quite loudly. Neeti remained calm and disconnected the call.

'What happened? Is everything alright?'

'Just a little fight; normal,' Neeti dismissed.

'Is it because of me?'

'Not just because of you.' Neeti pressed her lips. 'I will tell you about it...you were saying something about relationships and all. Complete that first.'

'I was saying that no relationship can work without certain compromises and adjustments. Not compromises actually...'

'Sacrifice is the word you are looking for,' Neeti smiled.

'Maybe.'

'You heard what Nitin was saying just now, didn't you?'

'Not clearly, but...I could hear my name. Do you fight often because of me? Does he have a problem with me staying here?'

'Will you move out if he does?' Neeti's eyes became cold. 'Or should I ask you to move out because he has a problem with that?'

'Maybe.'

'Should I also start going to temples every Sunday, start wearing saris every time I go out with him, become a little soft and the other hundred things he wants me to do or be? Should I?'

'If you love him, why not?'

'What is love, Dev? Do you even know?' Neeti folded her arms and leaned forward. 'What is it? And what is a sacrifice? Most importantly, why do I need either of these two things in my life?'

'To keep the loved ones happy; to keep yourself happy. I don't think you would feel good if you lose Nitin, would you?'

'I am going to use an extremely strange analogy here... don't laugh and take me seriously,' she said. 'Suppose I want a parrot and I go to the market to buy one. I wander around for hours and days but I find none. Then, after many days I see a sparrow and because either I am tired of all the search or I feel a sudden love towards it, I bring it home. After a few days, I realise I was looking for a parrot only. Would it be fair to start expecting that sparrow to be a parrot? Should I expect her to mimic one or suddenly become green and start eating chilies? That's what love is. In the end, we do come back to seek what we were always looking for. You cannot fool yourself into happiness with a sparrow for long, Dev. Your heart would keep coming back, wishing for a parrot.'

Neeti paused for a breath. 'I am almost 25. Within 2-3 years my parents will start asking me regarding marriage and I don't have any aversion to it. But, like any other girl, I always wanted to be with a guy of my choice. If, to make a relationship work, I have to compromise and adjust, or sacrifice, I might as well give the privilege of selecting that guy to my parents. I will make them very happy because I can try to change him into my parrot or try to change into a sparrow.'

Neeti moved closer to Dev, her hand waving right in front of him. 'There is no love at first sight, Dev; I don't believe in it. I feel it's gradual. We open ourselves to slide into it when we want, when we feel we are comfortable with it, when it comes to life. I believe in demanding my right from it instead of compromising with whatever it on offer. Who knows, it might falter and give me exactly what I am asking for, what I deserve, what I am worthy of. What will happen if it doesn't? I won't end up with nothing. No one does...I will compromise. But only then, Dev, only then.'

Dev looked into her sharp, confident eyes. He had nothing to say.

'I can bet Bhawna will be back in your arms in just two days if you try. She is just testing your patience, trying to make certain things clear to you. She is sending across a message, that's it. But I will not advise you to chase after a girl who cannot understand and appreciate you, Dev. Not anymore.'

Dev was surprised by the vehemence in Neeti's tone. What did that "not anymore" mean? It seemed like she was hinting at something. But then Neeti never willingly talked about his past life. Did her words have something to do with that? Dev didn't know how much he could agree with her. He still wanted Bhawna back, but he didn't want to disappoint Neeti at that moment; it was special.

He nodded and turned his face away; the questions in her eyes were too intense to be answered. He chose silence; missing the guidance he always sought, his mind already exploring the pages of that book, his story in Neeti's words.

Perhaps, the answers were in there…

# *CHAPTER 20*

Dev shut the door behind him and pulled out the thick file containing his memories from his bag once again. He sat on the bed and opened it. He had already marked certain page numbers, aspects of his life that needed to learn from, specific moments in his life that he had spoiled, like a beautiful relationship with someone whom he loved a lot.

*It's not easy for me to see Dev crumbling like this. He has done everything that he could for everyone, but I think that's not enough; after all, happiness is a costly thing. It will take a lot more out of him.*

*Dev came to see me. He tried to look happy, but also knew that he couldn't hide, not from me. He felt he was losing everything; I felt the same. I have felt the same for a long, long time, but I was always too weak to tell him that.*

*'I am a bad person,' he said.*

*'No Dev, you are just different. Naïve may be, but not bad.'*

*'I shouldn't have gotten into a relationship, if I couldn't live up to it.'*

*'But you are doing great.'*

*'You feel like that,' he shouted. 'You have always felt so, unfortunately not the woman I had made those promises to, not my parents, no one for that matter, except you. Kriti said she doesn't want this to work anymore.'*

*Dev turned his eyes from me.*

*'Why?'*

*'She said I am not giving her the attention she deserves. Perhaps, she is right. I am not. But I have other things to do. I want to take care of her as well. I don't know, Neeti; I am failing. I am failing everywhere.'*

*'No, you are not.'*

*'Stop saying that,' he shouted.*

*I was used to seeing him shouting at people who cared for him, but not like this. He wasn't like this.*

*'No one is happy with me, no one. Everyone feels I have become selfish.'*

*'What about you, Dev? Do you think that?'*

*'I feel nothing. I don't feel anything. Peoples' tears don't matter. Today, Kriti was complaining about me thinking about stuff that is not important, spending more time by myself rather than with her. She told me how she loved it when I wrote poems*

*for her and she asked me if I remembered the last time I had actually done that for her.'*

*'You haven't done a lot of things in a long time, Dev.'*

*'Those things mattered to the people around me, Neeti. Those people, who love me, who want to see me happy, but I am not sure whether I can keep them happy anymore?'*

*'Dev... don't think so much. Rest. You have lived for...'*

*'That's the biggest problem, Neeti. I am not thinking. I am not thinking about anyone. I am not even sure whether it matters to me, whether I even care about what matters to them. Something is happening...'*

Dev continued reading. The words seemed to point in one direction now – Bhawna. Every time Kriti's name came up on the page, Bhawna's image ran across his brain; his direction becoming clearer with every passing word.

*'Why are you doing that job without charging them, Dev? You are putting a hell of a lot of effort in it.' Kriti had used these exact words for the third time this month.*

*She had called me yesterday. I already knew about Dev's assignment. It was a small consultancy project that he had turned into a fortune changer for that company. He had approached the owner and promised to devote a couple of hours every weekend. No discussions regarding fee had taken place, but I knew Dev wouldn't charge anything.*

*'He is hiding it from his bosses at B&K and he has already made some 50 lakhs worth of profit for this company. I am not against him doing anything on the side. But he should be able*

*to demand what is rightfully his.' Kriti sounded worried. 'You know, Neeti, he is a little naïve when it comes to money. But you shouldn't allow someone to take advantage of you. I am tired of trying from my side. It was fine when he was doing it part-time, but now it's like he is working for both companies. Those people are making him work for 4-5 hours daily and he still doesn't ask for a single penny. I am concerned about his health, angry about the people exploiting him. What will he do in the future if things remain like this! And, he doesn't listen to anyone, at least not me anymore. I thought you might talk to him. At least, he values your opinion. I am treated like a fool. It's like his family and I are idiots.'*

*I told her I would talk to Dev, but I knew it was false hope that I shouldn't have given her. He wasn't going to listen to anyone, not till he was convinced that that was what he needed to.*

Dev sighed looking at his cell lying beside him. "One new message" flashed on the screen, as he turned it on. His fingers slid the screen open. It was Prashant; he had some things to discuss with him the next day. Little did it interest Dev. He turned his phone upside down and continued reading.

*'Why the hell can't I leave my job?' Dev shouted at Kriti.*

*It had been an hour since I had been trying to resolve the issue between them. Things were starting to go out of hand. Dev was feeling pressurised and yet, all parties concerned felt he didn't care. Even I didn't know if he actually cared.*

*'You are not thinking about the future Dev,' Kriti shouted.*

*I was a silent spectator, not a mediator anymore. Neither of them was ready to listen.*

*'Do you think I am an idiot to take such a big decision without thinking about the future?'*

*'I don't know, but you are arrogant enough to take decisions like this by yourself. It's about you and you only. Why can you not understand that your decisions impact me, impact your family. They impact many bloody other people, whom you never listen to.'*

*'Why should I? And why are you suddenly talking about my family and those "other people"? You never wanted me to listen to them in the first place and today you are using them to suit yourself?'*

*'Your family and I are on your side, Dev,' Kriti shouted.*

*Tears started flowing down her face, but they had little impact on Dev. She had burst into tears many times before in the last few weeks. I knew they wouldn't change anything.*

*'I have decided. I can only hope that you understand me.' Dev looked at me with eyes looking for only one thing – support. I don't know if I disappointed him.*

*'I am not going to change my mind,' he said and walked out.*

*He was well-settled in his firm and we also knew that he had outperformed everyone, and yet he chose to leave. He had his own reasons. It would have been easier had he shared them with everyone around him. I could cope with his behaviour, but could only hope that the others would as well. I feared that if things continued like this, he was never going to come back. I knew that he shouldn't be so harsh, ruthless; but he would always be the same sensitive guy he had once been.*

Dev skimmed through the next few pages. His pulse racing, a sense of urgency made him flip through the file; he felt as if he was missing something. He kept the book in his bag and left the apartment.

He knew what he had to do.

# *Chapter 21*

## 2 Days Later

'Bhawna,' Dev hailed her.

He knew that the terrace of the office was where he would find her. She heard Dev, her head tilted a bit as if in acknowledgement, but she knew she was strong enough not to give in at least at that moment.

She kept staring ahead; there was nothing there, but she could see all those special moments they had shared at this spot in the last few days. She took a small breath and forced her eyes shut; Dev held her hand already.

'Bhawna.' He stood beside her, her eyes still closed. 'I know what I did was wrong. I know there may be a lot of other things where I made some mistake or was going to make one. I don't have much to say, I just want to make up with you, tell you that I will try my best. I can't tell you how, but I do know what I have to do. I have always wished for you to be happy. I forgot that it was in my own hands to keep you so.'

Dev placed his notebook beside her, looked at her silent face and walked away.

Bhawna opened her eyes, as she felt his fingers brush her palm; tears streamed down her eyes. She stood there silently, lost, and then sat at their favourite table with the small notebook. There was nothing written in it, except the first page. She turned to the written words, shiny in the red brown ink, and started reading.

*my mind just woke up*

*from a long sleep*

*the dream was always true*

*that i could never see*

*but now i know that world*

*which we could never live*

*that love and that care*

*that i didn't try to give*

*i kept hoping it's not too late*

*i brought it home myself*

*and i saw it...only when you were gone*

*i will say just one thing*

*i won't call you back*

*i know i hurt you*

*i couldn't be what i said*

*sorry wouldn't be enough*

*maybe I didn't realise*

*without you, it'll be so tough*

Bhawna burst into tears. She hid her face in those pages. She took out her phone and called Dev. His phone rang once; she disconnected.

'I am bad,' she murmured and typed a text.

*Thank you. I overreacted I know, but you just made it all yours. You are amazing. Sorry.*

# CHAPTER 22

Dev came out of Prashant's cabin beaming. The day was turning into something better than he had expected. His boss had just had an hour long meeting with him regarding future prospects and other projects he had in store for him.

"It won't be just one, I can assure you. You will have to make a choice quick, really quick. You never know, tomorrow you might turn up at the office and the first thing I ask you to do is to pick your path ahead," Prashant had said.

There was no doubt that he was impressed; everyone was.

Dev took the stairs two at a time and went to the terrace. Bhawna's message brought another broad smile back on his face. He ran up two floors and slipped into the chair beside her.

'You aren't angry now?'

'No. I shouldn't have been that angry to begin with.'

'Well...you were right to be angry. I don't know how much but...'

'Dev, let's talk about something else. I don't want to discuss that fight.'

Dev smiled. His hand moved across the table to grasp Bhawna's restless fingers, to offer comfort. 'Prashant just told me that there are some really interesting projects coming up. He wants me to take up something big now, in a team obviously, but a smaller one. He said he will throw something big across my way pretty soon.'

'Do you really want it, Dev?'

'What? The project?'

'Yeah...but not just the project, this job as a whole. Do you really want it?'

'Well...I like it. I enjoy it.'

'But you haven't tried anything else. You might find other things better.'

'Perhaps. It's just that Neeti told me about how great I was at it and I thought...'

'But you could be equally good in other sectors. You chose this because Neeti told you you are good at it, Dev. It might have been a fresh start...'

'Maybe,' Dev mused. 'Neeti says something similar too. I was very curious to know what I was and...' He left his words hanging.

'I have seen you reading the newspapers, watching all

those news channels. I have seen you predicting the market so well, even though you know so little about it. Perhaps, you should give finance a shot.'

'Really? But why?'

'There is nothing in this line. I don't know how it was before, but I don't think the situation is great, financially. You are an MBA. You have a brand name. We have to be a little practical, Dev. We have to think about the future. I have been in this industry for quite some time and I know that it's not what it used to be.'

Dev kept looking at her face, the hand holding him tightly. He had questions. He wanted to ask about so many things but every word, every question was overpowered, suppressed by just one word by Bhawna – future.

It was the first time Bhawna had said anything about a future with him. It was the first time he felt she felt something serious for him. He was feeling a lot closer to her than he had ever been; more than he felt while kissing her, while holding her. He felt she was there with him and he also wanted to be right there.

'I will try. I will talk to Neeti as well.'

'I can try too,' Bhawna replied. 'My friend works at B&K. He says it's quite a good company and that they are looking for someone for their management profiles. In fact, the whole idea came to me after I talked to him.'

Dev's thoughts stopped for a second. He kept staring at Bhawna's happy face, his eyes numb, his thoughts in another time. His mind certain of one thing – he was being tested; he was being given a chance to atone for all that he had done in his past. Perhaps B&K was the answer, maybe then Bhawna and Neeti would see that he had changed.

## *CHAPTER 23*

### 5 DAYS LATER

Dev set aside Neeti's laptop and switched on the television. He had never thought he would dare intrude on another's privacy to such an extent. From the time he knew nothing about himself to today, when he knew a little bit, he had learnt a lot of things about himself along the way.

He cursed himself for having gone through each and every file in Neeti's laptop, but he had to do so. He had been forced to break his rule; he had never wanted to intrude on Neeti's privacy, but her reticence had forced his hand, first in downloading the folder in his name and now more than that. And all he had after that were more questions and a sense of betrayal so deep that it cut to his core.

*"Why!"* Dev thought, his gaze on the paper in his hand; a letter with his photograph.

He had received it from Bhawna's friend this morning. He folded it and kept it in his pocket as the door opened.

'Hi Dev,' Neeti came in. The black formals adorning her sleek body, as always. Dev smiled and switched the TV off.

'Neeti, I need to talk to you,' he said, struggling to remain calm.

'Can I change first?' Neeti stopped at the door to her room.

'It's not that urgent, but I am a little anxious...'

Neeti walked back to the living room and sat on the table in front of him. She could see the flush on Dev's face deepening. He was biting his lip, his eyes moving away from her; something was really bothering him.

'Is everything alright, Dev?'

'No,' he rushed the words out, before he could change his mind, 'I don't know where to begin.'

'Is everything fine between you and Bhawna?'

'Yeah... great actually. Everything has been pretty smooth since that day,' he paused, his body becoming more restless with every passing second.

'What is it, Dev? What happened?' Neeti asked.

'Bhawna suggested that I change my job.'

'So?'

'She said I should try my hand at something else, finance perhaps. She has seen how I keep a tab on the markets and says that my reading of the sensex is good.'

'Is that the only reason?' Neeti leaned forward.

'She was talking about a future,' Dev forced a faint smile on his face. 'Our future...she said there isn't much scope for money in this industry and...'

'And that you can earn much more in finance, that it will be good for both of you and your still unborn children.'

Neeti leaned back, folding her arms in front of her.

'It's not always about the money, Dev. I told you; don't run after a girl who cannot respect your professional goals and aspirations.'

'But what is wrong with me moving to some other company?' Dev's voice was rising with every word.

'Nothing wrong, Dev. It's just that you should like the work as well. There is a difference between keeping tabs on something and actually working in that industry. It is okay to jump sectors, but don't you think it is equally good to show some staying power in a particular field? Dabbling in something once in a while is completely different from seeing it, feeling it and experiencing it day in and day out.'

'But you told me yourself that I should take this life as a clean slate and experience and explore new things in it. This is also a direction to explore, right? How do we know whether I will like it or not, if I never give it a shot? I mean I have never worked in a finance company before. Maybe I should give it a shot this time around and see where it takes me?'

'Don't play with your life like this, Dev. You are a marketing genius. I know you miss being here. You have always loved your job. It's only because of that girl that you are thinking like this. You are happy in your job otherwise, aren't you?'

'That I was always happy in marketing doesn't mean I will be unhappy in accounting. Does it, Neeti? Or do you know something that you aren't telling me?'

Dev's voice had hardened; his eyes wide. He had never seen Neeti so vehement about anything in his life before. The best he could get from her was "follow whatever direction he wanted". But Neeti was different today.

Neeti noticed the sudden change in his voice. His hesitation had turned into something else; a belligerence of some kind, only she didn't know what.

'What is going on?' She asked, bewildered. 'Is this what you wanted to talk about, Dev? Or is something else the matter?'

'Why did you lie to me? Why are you lying to me even now? I am a finance geek, right? I have worked my entire life as an investment banker.'

'No, you are a marketing geek who was mistakenly understood to be a finance person by everyone, including yourself. There was no point telling you the truth, Dev. It would've only misled you. I told you what you needed to know.' Neeti remained calm, even as she braced herself for his questions, his anger.

'Did I even work in any of those companies?'

'Yes, I am not a liar, Dev. I just didn't tell you the complete truth. And the only reason I did not do that is because I felt you didn't need to know it. You were planning to leave your company anyway. You had been giving free consultancy to all your marketing clients for over a year. What was the point of telling you your real professional background then? I only told you what you wanted to become, pointed out your true calling. What you actually wanted to do.'

'I had the right…you should have…'

'I didn't want to confuse you, that's all. My intentions weren't to misguide you. I was...'

'I trusted you,' Dev shouted.

'How did you learn?' Neeti asked.

'Someone told me at work. Someone from B&K recognised me. And I am not sorry that I went through your laptop...'

Neeti took a deep breath. 'So you still want to try your hand at finance? Again?'

'Yeah,' Dev replied. 'I have this feeling that I was wrong the last time. Maybe I wanted to leave the company but...I might have been making a mistake. I want to give it another shot.'

'Don't do that, Dev. I have always supported you in whatever you have wanted to do in your life, but this time, you are wrong. You are making a choice because Bhawna is asking you to. And also because I lied to you. But these aren't the right reasons for you to change anything in your life.'

'They are not,' Dev mumbled and got up.

Dev knew he wasn't lying. The real reason behind that decision lay deep in his mind. It wasn't resentment, nor love; it was redemption, a consequence of his own actions based on words written in that file, that diary exploding inside his mind continuously. It was those words that were forcing him to take this path, a path that he had refused to choose in his first life, a path that could've made the many people in his life then a lot happier.

Dev was trying to live for those who weren't with him now.

## *Chapter 24*

**1 WEEK LATER**

'I thought I would give you a surprise by giving you all these options, but you've surprised me, Dev,' Prashant said, keeping the hard copy of Dev's resignation on his table, '…again.'

'Well…it came as a surprise to me also, Prashant. I thought I shouldn't leave such an opportunity.' Dev smiled at him, confidently.

Prashant scratched his cheek and got up. 'This is your final decision? You have thought through the pros and cons?'

'I've made up my mind.'

'Okay,' Prashant opened the door. 'Join me for a smoke, will you?'

'Sure,' Dev followed him.

Both men were on the terrace within seconds. The butt end of the pale white cigarette stick was in Prashant's hand, lit at the other end. The exhaled smoke blowing in the soft breeze of that slightly misty evening. Prashant turned to Dev with his eyes smiling silently.

'It's good that you submitted your resignation today,' Prashant took a long drag, realising that Dev had finished all his work on the Rang De project. 'You were sort of without work for the last 4-5 days. I can relieve you tomorrow, if you wish.'

'I would be glad, Prashant. Thanks for that.'

Prashant tapped the butt with his thumb to dust the ash. 'I don't have such conversations with everyone who leaves this company, but I felt that you should know something. I have a great fondness for you professionally because there was something different about the way you had introduced yourself to me. I wouldn't want you to make wrong choices in your life.'

'I think...'

'Listen...'

He smiled, as Dev folded his arms in a defensive manner but stood silent.

'Have you seen our company logo, Dev? Ever wondered what it tries to say?'

'Yes...I was wondering one day if that bird was trying to sit on the waves or trying to fly away from them.'

'Good. See that's why I have that attachment I was talking about.' Prashant paused to take another long drag. 'That bird is actually flying away. Doesn't matter how beautiful those waves or trees might seem to me and you, the bird will only and always use them to rest. Her actual place is out there… in the sky. In the end, she won't be happy on top of the water or inside that beautiful forest. That's what I wanted this firm to be – a place where birds can come to fly. I never looked for someone who may find his tree here, it was always a place to take some rest and move on.'

'I hadn't come here for just some rest. That was not the plan.'

'I am not saying that either. What I am trying to say is that if you ever feel that you have gone ahead only to find yourself sitting on the waves instead, you can always come back and explore your sky. I think all humans are smartest at the time of their birth. We are committed and focused when we are children but lose that focus along our way in this world. It becomes difficult to concentrate when there are so many roads ahead. When I was studying in grade 12, I had Maths, Physics, Chemistry, Hindi and English as subjects. I scored 76 percent marks, decent for that time. But you see, most of it came from Hindi; I scored 91 in it. Do you think I was happy to see that?'

'No.' Reply was reflexive.

'Exactly.'

Prashant took out a paper from his pocket. He unfolded it and held it towards Dev; it was his resume, the same that Dev had given Prashant.

'I made a mistake when you gave it to me. I thought I

would rectify it. I had told you that I would like to see many achievements on the front side of this page after a year or so,' Prashant paused. 'But I forgot that simple tasks can be much more important than achievements sometimes. I would have been much happier had I scored 85 in Math and 60 in Hindi even if that meant my percentage would come down. I know what I want to write on my front page. I hope and wish you don't find any of your achievements written on it to be meaningless, ever. Make wise choices in life, Dev. All the best.'

Prashant threw the cigarette butt on the ground and stubbed it.

'Thanks.'

Dev silently folded the resume and kept it back in his pocket. The front was still blank, as it had been a few weeks back. But Dev knew what Prashant had been trying to tell him: It was better to leave it blank than to fill it with something that he couldn't be proud of.

Dev had always known that to be so. He just didn't know if he was following that principle truly.

# *Chapter 25*

## Four weeks later

'Yeah, almost there, sweetie.' Dev disconnected the call and got up from the bench in the darkest corner of the small park.

It had been three weeks since he had joined his new, but old, company B&K. Things had changed a lot in the last few days. It seemed as if his whole life had changed, that he had changed.

"Why don't you move in with me," Bhawna had asked him fourteen days ago.

"I like to stay with Neeti. She has been an amazing, supportive friend. It wouldn't be nice to leave her like that," he had replied, but he also knew that those were going to be his last days at that apartment with Neeti. His life was fully reserved for his office and Bhawna now.

Neeti had now become a colleague, but no one could take her place; he knew it, she knew it and maybe so did Bhawna. It hadn't mattered to Neeti whether it was right for Dev or not; he always had her support. In fact she had even recommended his name for an investment profile in her firm. Dev was working adjacent to her office now.

He walked to his new apartment, a couple of steps away from the park, and stopped in front of the pot-holed road. There were puddles and clogging in the middle, the water glistening in the yellow light of the street lamp, reflecting the half-shadow of the moon.

He stepped onto the dirty street and stood silently, smiling, lost in his thoughts. He didn't know what pleasure that act gave to him apart from soaking his trousers and filling his shoes with muck, but he felt happy, complete, as if it was mud that had been missing from his life all this while; it was the mud that brought meaning to his routine, unexciting life of the past three weeks.

'Oh my God!' Bhawna jumped back as she opened the door. The floor outside was wet.

'Did you do that intentionally, Dev?'

She took in the evenness with which the mud covered his shoes.

'It was intentional,' he replied, taking his shoes off. 'I will leave them outside.'

This exact moment had been his reward for several days now. The smile on Bhawna's face had never been larger; she was happy, happy to be with him and his eccentricities, patient with his whims. It felt as if he had grown up, matured suddenly. It felt as if they had been together for years and not a few months.

'What is it?' he asked, stepping out of the bathroom after rinsing his feet and hands; Bhawna had already arranged the table.

'I need a favour and I have a good news,' she smiled.

'The favour first.'

'Both are one thing only.' She turned and kissed him on his cheek. 'Two in one.'

'You remember my cousin Sandhya?'

'Roshni of her office, right?'

'Yeah...the dumbo. She is looking for a job and wants to get into finance.'

'So?' Dev asked.

'So?' Bhawna pushed him slightly. 'So I told my parents that I have a great friend who can take her in and...' She paused, trying to contain her excitement. '...and Dev, this way my superhero friend will get a straight entry into my family's heart.'

Dev froze. He was experiencing one of those moments where his heart refused to accept a proposal that seemed reasonable in terms of personal gains. Everything was perfect about what Bhawna had just said. The favour guaranteed the cousin a good job, him a future that he had started dreaming about and Bhawna the happiness Dev had promised her. Except that something didn't feel right to him.

'I will talk to Neeti,' he said, his face lacking the excitement on Bhawna's face. 'I will see what can be done. Maybe we can get her an interview.'

Bhawna tried to stop herself from shouting; irritated, she said, 'She will come in at a very junior level, Dev. You don't need to talk to Neeti about that. You can pull it off yourself. Why an interview? You can just get her through, can't you?'

'But that's what I will talk to her about…'

'What?' Bhawna looked at him.

There were just the two of them at the table, yet Dev could feel the sudden silence like another person in the room. He set down the spoon. The conversation demanded eye contact.

'Who is Neeti to tell you what to do? Why do you need to consult her?' Bhawna pressed.

'I consult her on every important thing, Bhawna. You know that.'

'And all she does is manipulate you.' Bhawna snapped.

'Neeti is not the issue here. I don't feel comfortable with this idea of taking your cousin in just to impress your parents.'

'But...'

'In spite...' Dev forced his words out. 'In spite of knowing that she is not a deserving candidate. That is my problem.'

'How do you even know that?'

'You have told me yourself. You have always made fun of her.' He picked up the spoon again. 'You have compared her to Roshni yourself. Now, just because it's an opportunity for me doesn't mean that I recruit her or influence someone else to recruit her for a job which she is clearly unfit for. It would be unreasonable.'

'Unreasonable!' Bhawna screamed, stood up and pushed her chair aside. 'Unreasonable is you showing me this uncalled for attitude, Dev, knowing how important it is for me and for us.'

'Bhawna, try to understand...'

'No Dev, you try to understand. I am not asking you to rob your company. It's a perfectly reasonable favour because you are putting in a lot of effort into that company. If you have the authority to do something like this, then what is wrong?'

'If my company gives me some responsibility, they give it with a certain trust and expectations. How can my bringing in someone who clearly doesn't deserve that position be correct? It won't be fair to others working around her. It won't be fair to others trying to get that job.'

'Even you being in that company is not fair then,' she lashed out and left the room.

'I went through every single round of interview,' he murmured, eating again.

But Dev again had this nagging sensation that something was very, very wrong…

*'Help me... someone... anyone… please.' Dev was running in*

*that thick jungle once again, trying to save his life.*

*He felt like he had been chased for hours now, yet he didn't know what was following him. He didn't know what it wanted. He ran across the mud, everything invisible, yet present. He fell beside the large tree which appeared out of nowhere. He was panting badly, sweating.*

*Drops of water fell down on the black soil beneath him. He looked towards the sky which was shining bright even in that darkness. There were no clouds; there was no rain and yet the droplets. He looked down again; water was falling even now, burying him inside the death pool it had created. He brushed his hands across his face; it was wet, soaked, maybe in his own tears.*

*'There is no way out,' a voice reverberated around him.*

*'I will not die here,' he shouted, as colours prevailed around him again.*

*It seemed as if his voice had been heard by someone. The place illuminated in the brightness of day. He was standing in a room surrounded by people, all looking at him.*

*'What about the death we face every day, Dev?'*

*A lady walked towards him. He couldn't see her face, it was blurred, but he could feel her presence inside him, her voice more familiar than his own. She was sweet; there was agony in her tremulous voice, tears in those fogged eyes.*

*'Have you ever thought about how your father and I died for you every day for the last so many years, again and again, just to see you happy? But today it doesn't matter to you if we actually die...' The lady became louder.*

*'It doesn't matter. I have taken a decision. I am not helping him.' Words slipped out of his mouth. He didn't know what they were talking about, yet he knew he was a part of that conversation. He knew what his role was, what he had to deliver.*

*'He is your brother.' The lady was becoming louder with every word. 'We brought you up so that one day you would support your family. So that one day, you would help everyone around you. But you have become selfish. You have started showing your power and position to us, your own family.'*

*'Think whatever you like,' Dev uttered monotonously. 'I have made up my mind. I am not taking him in. He does not deserve to be at that position.'*

*'I know these are not your words.' The words were loud enough to shake him this time. 'It's that girl misguiding you. You were not like this. You used to love us. You never said no to your mother like this.'*

*The pounding voice inside his head made the words echo in his head; the noise becoming unbearable.*

'Bhawna,' he opened his eyes and shouted. The TV was loud, the lurid Bollywood song playing in front of his eyes annoying him.

'Bhawna,' he shouted again, his hand seeking the remote.

'Sorry.' Bhawna came in and shut the TV.

He held her hand and pulled her close. He turned his gaze to the file peeping out from the bottom of his pillow; the entire dream played through his mind.

'I will talk about your cousin. I will talk to someone to

take her in.'

Dev kissed Bhawna on the forehead. His words, slightly broken, reached Bhawna's ears.

She burrowed her face in his shoulder, a quiet but triumphant smile on her face; a smile that Dev didn't see, a smile that showed that she believed that she had won, the one that showed that Neeti had lost.

'You are amazing, Dev,' she said, kissing him; tears of gratitude shone in her eyes. She hugged him hard and slipped into the bed beside him.

All was okay in Bhawna's world...

# Chapter 26

Dev had been wandering on the road for hours now. Lost in thought, he didn't realise how many times Bhawna had already called. His phone rang again as he continued walking on the deserted road, but the sound finally caught his attention.

'Yeah, Bhawna,' he said.

'Where are you? Why were you not picking my call? Do you have any idea how worried I am?' Bhawna yelled.

'I am sorry. I didn't realise. My phone was on silent.'

'When are you coming back?'

'In 5-10...'

He stopped to take in the night around him. The area was familiar, yet not the place he should've headed. He had been walking for a long time. He looked towards a building, baffled; within a few seconds his eyes confirmed it. He was close to his old apartment, the one he had shared with Neeti. The lights were on; Neeti was probably home already.

'I am not coming home today,' he muttered. 'I'm going to see an old friend.'

Dev disconnected the call without waiting for Bhawna to respond. He could picture her shocked face, her frustrated anger. He knew she would call again and knew that what he was doing would only make matters worse, yet he switched off his phone and walked inside the building.

'Hi,' Dev smiled, as Neeti opened the door. She looked at him surprised for a few seconds and then walked back inside silently.

Neeti flopped on the sofa, her skinny legs, uncovered till mid-thigh, placed on the table. She switched off the TV and beckoned to Dev. 'Welcome home again!'

Dev sighed. 'It is home.'

He sat on the sofa and removed his shoes. 'I miss this place.'

The apartment had a positive air; he felt as if he had never left it, as if he should never leave it again.

Neeti, in her light pink tee-shirt and matching shorts, was looking pretty like she always did, but it was the first time he realised how soothing her presence had always been.

'So what's wrong?' she asked.

'Hey...just because I've come to see you doesn't mean that something is wrong. I just thought I would come and see you.'

'Does she even know that you are here, Dev?'

'Did she call you?'

'No,' she replied, taking her feet off the table. 'But your phone is off.'

Dev looked at the cellphone in his hand, smiled and kept it on the table. He turned his head towards Neeti again; both of them kept smiling, no words; none were required.

'What happened, Dev?' she asked again. 'I could see something was wrong today, even at the office. I was going to talk to you.'

'I don't know,' he sighed, 'I am just trying to keep her happy, but...it's stupid. I get confused over petty things. Bhawna asked for a small favour and…I mean she is my girlfriend. We are talking about our future, so it's not even a favour…It's sort of a family responsibility or something…'

'What favour?'

'She wanted me to hire her cousin. I talked to Pranab and he said he would.'

'Why are you feeling bad about it then? She was looking for a job and you helped her. It's a good deed, I believe.'

'She doesn't deserve it. I have talked to that girl and I have heard Bhawna talking about her many times. She doesn't deserve to be there. She will not do the work required.'

'Many people in this world are paid for doing things they are not fit for. There are thousands out there who do not deserve to be at their jobs; there are thousands others who do not put in the effort required after reaching where they wanted to. So another one did. What's the big deal?'

'It matters to me, Neeti. If it was in my hands, I would take back the opportunities from all those people and give them to those who actually deserve it, who actually slog for it, put up a fight for it. If that is not in my hands, I should do justice to at least those things that actually are in my reach. There might be some really intelligent college student slogging his ass off to get the job which I just handed out to a girl who might not give even her twenty percent to it.'

'Then why the fuck did you?' Neeti's voice changed. Expressions on her face changed; the smile faded and her eyes, firmly fixed upon his face, penetrated his soul.

Dev felt like she was talking to a criminal. He had never seen that face. He had never heard that voice. He knew it was a different Neeti he was talking to. Her voice low, yet intimidating.

'Bhawna asked me and...'

'And you couldn't refuse?' Neeti leaned forward. 'Maybe you were right, Dev, maybe I was wrong. Maybe I should have told you everything about your past. It would have been much better had I misled you by mistake than to see that girl misleading you by force.'

'She is not...'

'Let me finish...she *is* forcing you. I have been telling you that she's not the right girl for you, Dev. You can't keep doing things just to make her happy. Maybe you should concentrate on yourself for a change. If you can share your thoughts so clearly in front of me, why can't you do the same in front of her? You have always wanted to know how you were, right? I will tell you. The old Dev I knew would never ever have accepted such a thing.

'I know. Maybe I was wrong in doing that. I don't want to be wrong again.'

'Do you feel as if you are wrong in denying her, Dev?' Neeti became louder. 'Or do you feel you are wrong in doing whatever you did today? Do I need to respond to that stupidity? You can write a fucking thesis on unethical favours, but you go ahead and do just that because you had to make Bhawna happy?'

'I want this relationship to work, Neeti. I just want to see her smiling all the time.'

'Even if she demands something wrong? What if she asks you to stop seeing me? Or do fraud in your company to earn more money? I am not saying that she would demand any of these things, but there has to be a line where you stand up and say to her that she is wrong, that it is unacceptable.'

'I don't know...' Dev sighed.

'It would have been different had you been confused, but this time you are amazingly clear. You knew you were going to do something wrong and you went ahead and did it anyway. Why can't she understand that some things might trouble you as well, Dev?' Neeti sat beside him and held his hand. 'You have as much right to be happy as she does and she has exactly the same responsibility towards keeping you happy as you have to her...'

Dev kept staring deep at Neeti's concerned eyes. Once again, he didn't know if he was going to follow any of her advice, but he knew that those eyes reflected only concern for him. He knew that they meant him well. He knew the only thing that mattered to Neeti was him and his happiness. Perhaps that is why he was here with her like this rather than with Bhawna. He needed this, needed to know that he was not alone in his thinking.

Dev shut his eyes and turned his face away from her. He knew his actions had made Bhawna happy, but he wasn't sure he felt the same about them.

'I have always believed one thing, Dev. You are only happy if those you love are. That's why you try to keep Bhawna so happy. Her smile makes you feel special. What you did will make her feel like an angel, but if you don't like it, either you don't love her or you have done something terribly wrong.'

Dev remained silent as the words wounded his heart. He opened his eyes and saw Neeti's face with his astounded eyes. He gulped a deep breath and switched his phone on.

'You are right. Let's sleep. I will talk to Bhawna tomorrow,' he said, stood up and walked into his old bedroom.

Bhawna opened the door as the bell rang for the third time. She kept staring at Dev as he walked in silently, placed his bag on the chair and walked to the kitchen. She closed the door and followed.

Dev took out a water bottle and returned to the dining area, still no words. Bhawna's breathing became heavier; she had been expecting something, an explanation, a fight, but all she saw in Dev's eyes was hatred, as if he had been forced into the house by someone.

That someone couldn't have been anyone but one person; she knew it. She hated her influence on Dev; she disliked the fact that he went to her for everything…what was this hold she had on him? Why was Dev not totally hers? Would he ever solely be with her?

'You could've told me that you were going to see Neeti,' she broke the silence.

'It was all of a sudden,' he replied, his eyes still on the table.

'What happened?' Bhawna uttered in exasperation. 'I cannot run after you, begging you to tell me your problems all the time, Dev. It would be easier if you could tell me yourself.'

'And what difference would it make?' Dev turned towards her, his face stoic, eyes cold, words stiff. He knew what was ahead; he had given up on being heard, even though he hadn't even tried.

'Dev!'

Bhawna looked at him aghast. Dev's words had surprised her. She had been arguing with herself for the last twenty odd hours. She had lived this fight, imagined their argument from every angle possible, trying to fit in her role in various situations, yet these words had never been part of any scenario she had envisioned. She had failed to see them coming. Dev had left her speechless.

'I talked to my colleague regarding your cousin,' Dev said.

'He said she would get the job, but I am not going to send him her resume. I've decided not to.'

Bhawna kept looking at his expressionless face. She could see Dev was determined, more than ever she had seen him. There was an unusual strength in his words.

She knew where that had come from. She snapped, 'Neeti suggested that, didn't she?'

'No,' Dev replied. 'I did, but she supported me...'

'The way I should have?'

'Yes.'

'Can't you see what she is doing, Dev? Or you don't want to?'

Bhawna's angry words shocked Dev. He looked at her with scorn. He couldn't believe that Bhawna didn't understand, he refused to believe what she was saying.

'That bitch is manipulating you,' Bhawna screamed. 'That's what she has been doing from the beginning, Dev. She loves you and can't see you happy with me.'

'Have you gone mad?' Dev yelled back. 'You have no idea what you are talking about? I am alive only because of that girl. She had complete control over my life. I was in her hands when I woke up all alone in that hospital. I kept asking her about my past life, still do and still she didn't do anything. She could have said anything to me and I would have believed her, but she told me to write my own destiny. You know nothing about her, Bhawna, so think twice before speaking out against her. She has always thought about my best unselfishly. No one in this world can do what she has done. Not even you.'

'This is exactly how she has got to you, Dev. She wanted to become the girl whom you turn to every time, just like you did yesterday. She never counted on your meeting me and now she is poisoning your mind against me. She even showed you that fake boyfriend and broke up with him the moment you fought with me. She has made you so blind to anything else that you can't see what is real. She has been playing this game since the beginning, Dev. You and I are fighting because of her, for God's sake!' Her voice broke.

'We are fighting because of your cousin, not Neeti,' Dev said coolly. 'But you won't understand. There is a huge difference between you and her, Bhawna. She doesn't think that you stole me from her, even though you may have. Even today, she said hiring your cousin would make you happy and that would make me happy. But I don't want to. Do you understand?'

Dev walked towards the main door, unperturbed by her tears.

'I can't always be wrong, Bhawna; you can't always be right. I made the mistake of pretending that it was okay, though.' Dev turned the knob, opened the door and walked out.

Bhawna didn't follow him. She didn't stop him. She knew he wouldn't listen to her, but she wasn't done. Dev may have been right, but she felt she wasn't wrong either.

'I will prove to you that Neeti is wrong for you, Dev. Just wait and see...'

# *Chapter 27*

## 3 DAYS LATER

'What now?' Dev shouted.

It had been three days since he and Bhawna had fought. And suddenly that afternoon, Bhawna had appeared in front of Dev's office. Soon he was in her car, travelling to some undisclosed destination. Bhawna had asked him to come with her, that it was really urgent, and he had agreed.

But he had had enough. Bhawna wasn't saying anything and he wanted to know what was going on.

'Bhawna!' Dev shook her shoulder, but she continued driving. 'Why won't you tell me where we are going? You are scaring me now.'

'My home,' she replied.

Dev could tell that something was amiss, he could sense urgency on her face; something was not right.

'Why?'

'I want you to meet someone,' she replied without looking at him.

Dev realised they were a couple of minutes away from the apartment.

'Who?' He took a deep breath.

Bhawna turned towards him. 'I am sorry. I really am. But after that fight, I sort of lost my trust in Neeti and I started doubting you as well. I spied on you.'

'What?' Dev almost shouted. 'How could you?'

'I am really sorry, Dev, but I was checking everything. I went to the hospital and hired some professionals as well. I just wanted to prove to you that Neeti is not a good girl; that she is trying to do something really wrong and...'

'Stop the car.' Dev forced the words out. 'Stop it. I came with you because I thought this was serious, but you are talking the same crap. And you spied on us? On her? Have you gone mad?'

Bhawna stopped the car. They had reached the apartment. 'Dev, listen to me.'

Dev opened the door and jumped out. Bhawna stepped out to follow him, but Dev had started running.

'Dev!' she shouted, her voice as loud as possible. 'I found your parents. I found your father,' she paused, '...and mother.

They are there in my apartment, waiting for you.'

Dev froze, as her voice reached his ears. He turned to look at the face of the woman who had dared to play with his past, but there was no deceit on that face nor malice; Bhawna was not lying. He could see that. He walked up to her silently and they moved towards the elevator.

'Stay strong. Your mom's been crying since morning. Don't...'

'How…' Scattered words came out of his mouth.

Bhawna couldn't hear anything, but she decided to stay silent. She held his hand and walked with him to the flat. With a click she opened the door; an old lady in her mid 50s was sitting in the chair, a tall lean man of almost the same age standing behind her. Both looked towards her awestruck, as she walked in with Dev after her.

'Dev!' The woman burst into tears as Dev stepped inside.

She ran to Dev and embraced him at once; her face soaking his shirt with tears, her arms trying to gather as much of him as possible in their fold.

'*Deva!* It's you, my son. We've found you,' she sobbed.

Dev could sense the tremor in her voice. The voice seemed strangely familiar to him, as if he had heard it sometime, somewhere in his past.

Tears blurred his vision. He could barely make out the lean figure of the man, standing behind so far, coming towards him. He might never recognise his face, but he had seen that hazy image in his dreams.

Could it really be? Were his parents truly alive? Had Neeti lied to him? Was what Bhawna was saying true? The tears in the eyes of the woman who held him seemed real, but why would Neeti hide them from him? What was going on? He couldn't believe that the woman who had supported him all this time had betrayed him. He had seen genuine concern in her eyes, felt her anger at him being forced to do things he felt were wrong. How could that woman, his Neeti, his best friend, betray him so?

He didn't know what to believe anymore. He needed to know…

'Coming!'

Neeti switched off the TV and went to the door as the bell rang again. Whoever was outside was in real hurry. She opened the door; a hand flew fast into her face.

The sound of the slap reverberated across the corridor; Neeti's face turned red. She kept looking at the floor for a few seconds, reeling at what had just happened. She had barely made out the person who had hit her. She didn't say a word and retreated into her apartment slowly.

'We treated you like a daughter,' Mrs. Sareen shouted at the door.

Mr. Sareen was holding his wife's hand. He knew her rage wouldn't end at just one slap.

'How could you do this to us?' the woman screamed again.

Neeti stood silently.

'I am not coming in,' Mrs. Sareen vented. 'I didn't even

want to see your face. But Dev wanted to see you, so I came here one last time. Satisfied no, Dev?' she said, 'Son, we'll wait downstairs. Don't take long.'

Neeti didn't move as the duo walked away. It was just Dev in front of her, mute, astounded, betrayed, torn.

Neeti turned to look into his eyes. There was something different about them that day; there wasn't the innocence with which Dev used to look at her, that trust with which he told her everything, with which he had made her his mentor. Her lips quivered, but her eyes refused to give up.

'I am back in the same place where I was a few months back, Neeti.' Dev walked towards her deliberately, his eyes fixed on her face. 'Do I know anyone? I am all alone.'

'I am with you,' she murmured.

'Still? You were talking to them all this time, weren't you? You were talking to my parents while I was lying in my room thinking that they had all died, thinking that I must have done something terribly wrong to deserve this.'

'Dev,' her voice trembled for the first time since he had walked in the door.

'I won't ask why. I only came to tell you that I am leaving with them. I couldn't leave like this, without saying goodbye despite everything…'

'Maybe someday you will ask...'

Neeti wiped the tears in her eyes. Her face was still red, but showed no remorse.

Dev shook his head and walked back to the door. The bag on his shoulder slipped to his arm; he stopped and turned. 'I just want to know,' he said, taking the thick file out of his bag. 'I found this in your laptop. I've been trying to redeem myself since then. This isn't fake, right?'

Neeti opened the file and turned the pages. The words inside were familiar; too close to her to be forgotten. She looked at Dev.

'I am not the only one to hide things,' she said, sadly. 'Every word in it is true, but only if you choose to see it.'

She opened Dev's bag and placed the book inside, her hand brushing over his arm, her fingers aching to touch him one more time, but she stopped herself. Now was not the time. He was too angry. He wouldn't understand why she had kept such important things from him. Maybe in time…

'Keep it with you, Dev. Some things must always be remembered, while others are not memorable at all. I am sure you hate me, want to forget me now, but I don't want you to forget this diary,' she said, trying to put a brave face on. 'Don't lose this chance to redeem yourself. Just don't.'

Dev looked at her face one more time; it still had the same faith in him. He turned his gaze, unable to take in what he saw in her eyes in the face of what he saw as her betrayal. Neeti had only love and concern for him, but he couldn't trust it, he couldn't trust anyone now; she had taken that from him and for that he didn't think he would ever be able to forgive her.

Dev blinked in disbelief and walked out. Neeti kept looking at him.

The door remained open and she was alone in the apartment once again.

For the first time in her life, she was scared to close that door.

## *Chapter 28*

### 2 DAYS LATER

Dev turned his head towards the window of the white Tata Indica racing on the highway. His father looked at him from the rearview mirror; the happiness on his face slipped as he saw Dev's grimace in the sharp light of the street lamps. He kept staring at Dev, but the boy didn't move, his eyes didn't blink; he was quiet.

'Drive slower,' he told the driver.

'It's already slow, sir. Madam didn't let me go above 50,' the driver said, pointing towards Dev's mother sleeping in the back seat between Dev and Bhawna; tiredness had caught up in the eyes of both the ladies. 'If you don't allow me to drive at 80 on empty roads, we will only reach by tomorrow morning.'

Mr. Sareen didn't respond, his eyes were still fixed in the

mirror, on Dev who hadn't moved his head even now.

'Dev, are you awake?' Mr. Sareen chose to break the silence. The reply he wanted never came; Dev didn't utter a word, his eyes fixed outside, lifeless.

Only Dev knew what was going in his head; the only other person who could have dared peek inside it was not with him anymore; he had walked out on her hours back.

"Meerut 20 km", a broken blue board passed by as Dev continued exploring the empty space in front of his eyes. He had come a long way from Mumbai, a long distance away from all those memories given to him by Neeti; a lot closer to those which had been given by people he had forgotten.

It had been 16 hours since he had left Mumbai. They had travelled to Delhi, visited temples, bowed in front of unproven self-proclaimed human gods before hiring a taxi to their home – Meerut.

Dev rolled down the window slowly. The rush of air mixed with dust clung to his face at once. His eyes shrank; hurting, asking for rest, but Dev was adamant. He kept his eyes open even as the cold air kept pushing them shut.

'She cannot be this bad...' The words slipped out as his thoughts went to those beautiful moments spent with Neeti, and his heart continued to hurt from the inside.

'It's hard for us to believe that as well, son,' his mother's sleep heavy voice reached his ears. She had finally woken up.

Dev turned towards her. He hadn't expected anyone to hear him, to respond.

'She has kept us away from you for so long.'

A tear slid down her face. She touched Dev's head in wonder. Each second, each moment that Neeti had deprived her of her son reflecting in the pain in her voice.

Dev didn't say anything. Emotions had been raging inside his head for long, yet he kept a smile on his face and closed his eyes.

'We've reached, Sarala.' Another voice intervened.

Mr. Sareen looked back and smiled at the two. 'I thought you would be asleep,' he said.

'Maa was. I wasn't sleepy anyway.'

'You used to sleep a lot,' his mother replied. 'It used be so difficult for us to wake you up sometimes. Now you are back, I am sure you will get good sleep again.'

'Come out now, we will talk inside.' Mr. Sareen took the keys of the house and stepped outside to open the door.

Dev stepped out of the car in a small street in front of a not too big blue house. He kept looking at the house for some time; it didn't seem like his own. He felt like he had woken up from that horrible long sleep once again, like he had lost his memory once again and this time had no anchor. He turned to find Bhawna; at least one familiar face with him; he wasn't lost.

'Sarala,' Mr. Sareen called Dev's mother. 'You take the kids inside; I will pay the driver and come.'

Dev looked at his father, who was reaching for his wallet

and moved inside with his mother and Bhawna.

The house wasn't as small as it had looked from outside. There were three rooms; one of them his own. He turned towards his mother for an explanation, but she had already started preparing the bed.

'Won't you sleep with us, Dev?' Mrs. Sareen asked. 'It's been months since I talked to you. I won't let you sleep in your room. You can go there tomorrow.'

'Okay, Maa.'

Dev turned towards Bhawna, who was smiling looking at the two. Dev tilted his eyebrow suggesting that she come and sleep as well. Bhawna didn't reply and walked to Mrs. Sareen.

'You too, Bhawna,' Mrs. Sareen smiled looking at Dev and waved her over.

# *Chapter 29*

## 2 DAYS LATER

'*Behan ji*, no one can be trusted these days. First, I heard about Mrs. Thakur and now you.'

An unfamiliar voice woke Dev from his sleep. He opened his eyes and lay still. He was used to unfamiliar faces, voices, things now. It had become a part of his life. Everything and everyone was a stranger to him, more so now.

'I treated her like my own daughter, *Bhabhi ji*,' his mother's voice followed the unfamiliar voice; she was in tears again.

Dev was irritated, as he tried to hear what else was being said…the voices loud enough to carry to him; they were making no effort to speak softly.

'I know. I had seen her in your home so many times. She used to eat with you people, go out with you. Neeti, she is the same girl who made *rangoli* in your home on Diwali, right?'

'Yeah,' his mother was still sobbing.

'And she did this? Unbelievable!'

For some reason this made Dev angry. Before he could figure out why, he heard his mother again and opened his eyes in a very thin slit; he looked like he was still asleep.

'Come, *beta*,' his mother hailed Bhawna, as she walked in with the tea and snacks. 'Keep it here.' Mrs. Sareen pointed to the small table beside the bed.

Bhawna kept the tray on the table, looked at Dev's motionless body hopefully, faked a smile at his mother finding him still asleep and left the room. She had been waiting for Dev to get up for more than two hours now. His mother had asked her not to wake him up.

'Who is this girl, Sarala *behan ji*?' The intrusive lady asked, as Bhawna stepped outside.

'His girlfriend,' Mrs. Sareen replied.

'She seems to be a good girl.'

'Nah...' Mrs. Sareen was quick to reply. 'She is not good. She acts too much and doesn't know how to cook properly either. But we are fine now; at least she cares for Dev. She is the one who found us because she felt that Neeti was trying doing something wrong. She saved him, by God's grace, otherwise that witch would've never let us know.'

'She already did, *behan ji*.'

'I don't want any scenes this time,' Mrs. Sareen ignored

the lady. 'I never liked that other girl Kriti either because I thought she was taking advantage of Dev's innocence, but it turns out she wasn't that bad either. The main culprit was someone else, someone whom I trusted. I think I've grown old. I can't differentiate between a good and bad person anymore. It will be better to accept his choice this time.'

'Stop blaming yourself, *behan ji*. Anyone can fail to identify, if the enemy hides in your own house, being a family member.'

'Still I should've suspected before. He always did what we told him. He never disappointed us and then he changed; he was fighting with everyone. He stopped talking to me, didn't listen to his father. He was fighting with that girl also, but he never fought with Neeti. It never struck me that it was she who was playing games. She was manipulating my son and I was giving her more power over me. I always called her for help, sent Dev to her for guidance. I was the one to tell Dev that he should listen to her, even when he felt that we were stupid.'

Tears swelled in her eyes again. 'Dev is innocent, but we should've been more careful. She planned everything, *bhabhi ji*. She kept my son from me for thirteen months. How could she do that to us! I was talking to her on the phone all the time. She used to console me. She used to tell me that Dev must be angry and that is why he left home. I knew Dev couldn't leave us like that. I knew my son could not leave his home, his mother, just like that. Bloody bitch! She will go to hell. She will rot for ruining our lives.'

'Maaa...'

Mrs. Sareen's words pinched Dev's heart. He turned towards her slowly and opened his eyes. His mother was crying, but his reason for speaking up could not be ignored, at least not by him; it was difficult for him to hear anything against Neeti.

'Why are you crying?'

'Nothing, son,' his mother wiped her tears and sat beside him. 'I was just telling Rekha auntie about you. I didn't want to disturb your sleep.'

Dev kissed her hand gently and stood up. His bag was lying beside the bed. He picked it up and left the room without saying another word.

Dev went to the balcony and took the thick file out from his bag once again. He flipped through the pages and leaned forward on the railing. He didn't know whether to trust what was written in the diary in his hand, whether it was a collection of memories or steps of an elaborate plan laid out to string him like a puppet or something else, something Dev was yet to figure out.

'What is this, Dev?' Bhawna's voice snagged his attention.

She was standing beside him, staring at the file in his hand, not liking the stress on his face. Dev looked at and kept the file in the bag.

'No idea,' he said dismissively and walked inside the room. 'Come, I need to see my home.'

'Dev,' Mr. Sareen called him.

'Yeah,' Dev stood, seeing him. He was alone, waiting for Bhawna and Mrs. Sareen to return from the market.

'Sit, my son,' his father said. 'This is yours.' He placed a small notebook in his lap.

'Mine?' Dev picked it up and opened it curiously. The notebook was mostly empty, just a few pages filled. He quickly turned to the pages inked in blue and black. A small smile came on his face as he started reading; they were all poems.

'So I did write poems,' he said.

'I never understood how good these were while you were here with us. I even scolded you for writing these instead of focusing on studies.'

'Studies? How old is this book?' he asked, inspecting the book that didn't look very old.

'I think you started writing these during your graduation,' Mr. Sareen said, his voice heavy. 'But I want you to keep this today. You write well.'

'You read them all?' A wave of excitement thrilled him.

'Yes,' Mr. Sareen replied. 'I read them whenever I missed you…everyday.'

'Papa,' Dev said, the name still unfamiliar to him, and took Mr. Sareen's hand in his. 'I am here now.'

'But you will leave again,' Mr. Sareen turned his face, pale, towards him. 'Won't you?'

'Not forever, Papa.'

'Why don't you stay with us?' Mr. Sareen grasped Dev's hand firmly. 'You can get a job here. You can join your uncle's business. He is coming to see you this weekend and he always wanted you to join him.'

'But I didn't want to, right?'

'I don't know why. You never told us, but I am sure the reason is not there anymore.'

'I don't know why, Papa, but I feel that it's there. It's still there. I have to go back to Mumbai, to my job. I have already committed many things to Bhawna and she chose me even when I didn't have any family. She was all that I had, along with Neeti. Just because I have you people now, deserting her or asking her to compromise will be wrong.'

'We will talk to her, son. Can't you do this for us? We've been waiting to see you for so long. Don't put us through the same pain again,' Mr. Sareen's voice trembled. 'Please don't.'

Dev nodded.

A small smile came on Mr. Sareen's face; Dev forced one too, but his heart was already miles away...

## *Chapter 30*

## Next day

'Are you staying here, Dev?' Bhawna spoke, as Mrs. Sareen went to open the door, leaving the two of them alone for the first time in the day.

'Did my father say anything to you?' Dev kept the book on the table and asked.

'No, your mom did, when we were shopping. She said you would stay here with them, that you would find a new job here or...'

'Or join my uncle's company?' Dev completed.

'Yes, see Dev, I can't shift here. I have everything in Mumbai and so do you. It would be foolish to come here. What will we do here? Do you want me to become a housewife?'

'I didn't say yes, Bhawna. I am just thinking about it.'

'Thinking about it? How can you even consider this!' Bhawna asked quickly; Dev's mother was coming back. 'Can't we call your parents there instead? I am fine with that, but not with shifting here.'

Bhawna got up and went inside the kitchen, as Mrs. Sareen called his name. 'Dev, you have a guest, son. Don't talk to her for long. Tell her you are not well.'

'Who is it?' Dev asked, surprised.

'Kriti,' his mother replied.

Dev looked at his mother's face in awe. He couldn't stay any longer. He rushed towards the drawing room. A tall, beautiful girl in a blue *kurta* and black jeans was sitting there, her eyes fixed on the door.

She stood up as Dev rushed in, her gaze fixed upon him, acknowledging the presence of the person she had waited for, for so long. She kept looking at Dev for some time, her eyes taking in that it was the same person that she loved and lost months back, the same person who had changed her life, who had changed her.

'Kriti,' Dev said.

He forced himself to recall that face, but was disappointed; once again, she looked like any other stranger to him. He kept looking at her face. She was exactly how Neeti had described. Neeti had not lied about how she looked.

'You look amazing. I had an extremely beautiful girlfriend.'

'I heard you have one even now,' Kriti smiled and sat down again.

Dev took a seat in front of her. 'Bhawna is as beautiful as you are. You want to meet her?'

'No,' Kriti said, 'I mean yes, but not now. I have wanted to talk to you alone for some time now. I told your mom that also. It's been really long, you know.'

'Yeah,' Dev said, with a faint smile. 'I was wondering how come Maa was not here. She usually doesn't leave me alone. I didn't expect her to leave me alone with you for sure.'

'She was about to be my in-law, Dev,' Kriti smiled. 'I know how to handle her.'

The smile on Dev's face shrank at the last few words, the shine in his eyes faded. He took a deep breath.

'I want to apologise,' he said, looking down. 'I wanted to apologise to everyone but somehow I can't gather enough strength. I don't know how to, but seeing you has made me strong.'

'Apologise?' Kriti laughed. 'For what?'

'For not being what I promised,' he paused to look into her eyes. 'For hurting you again and again, for being rude, for having behaved the way I did and for...'

'Who told you that? You think you hurt everyone?'

'I know it,' Dev replied. 'I just know it. I know how I ignored every person's love and how I...but I am not that same person anymore. I have been trying to change, to be good. I wish I could change how I was in the past, but that is not in my hands.'

'Why didn't you come back to me then?'

'I...' Dev stopped, astounded.

'You got married, right? Neeti told me.'

'Otherwise you would've...' Kriti said, ruefully; the next words just slipped from her tongue, her voice lost in thought. 'Wow...that girl actually didn't tell you anything. I don't know where she gets the strength from to do these things. I respect her even more now. She has to be mad to go through everything that she has done alone, just for you. I wouldn't have been able to do it. I wouldn't...'

'What?' Dev's voice was low, surprised to hear such admiration in his ex's voice for his best friend, a friend he had walked out on thinking that she had betrayed him

'We had broken up two weeks before you left, Dev,' Kriti spoke. 'You had left your home, everyone and everything behind. I know because you had come to tell me, one last time. You had come to give me this.'

Kriti took out a small piece of paper from her purse and kept it on the table.

'I am not married, Dev,' Kriti whispered. 'But Neeti was right in lying to you because I know you would've come back to me after that accident or whatever it was, had she not lied to you. I hate her for snatching my only chance to get back with you, but she was right to do so. It would have been wrong to take advantage of you, but I would have done anything to keep you with me. I would never have told you that we had broken up…'

'I had…' Dev kept staring at her face, his head reeling. 'Why…'

Dev took a deep breath to collect himself and spoke, 'You know about Neeti? You've come here because of her, haven't you?'

'Yes,' Kriti said, 'I can't believe how a human being can be so selflessly dedicated to taking care of someone.'

'Taking care?' Dev's voice became loud, as he raged, 'she kept me from my family for so long. I used to cry at night, Kriti, thinking I must've done something horrible to see those days. I…'

'She kept you away from a family that you had chosen to leave, Dev,' Kriti snapped. 'She didn't want you to make a choice because of your emotional vulnerability. She knew you would've never gone back to them before achieving whatever made you leave them in the first place if you had your memories in place. She was only doing what you had already decided.'

'That decision was wrong. Like the one to break up with you, like the one to deny you happiness that I promised, like the one to not respect my own parents' wishes, their love, like many other decisions that I have made in my past…they were all wrong.'

'Who told you that you did that?'

'Doesn't matter.'

'It does, Dev. Because that person didn't tell you the whole truth. I hated you; I cursed you the way you are doing right now.' She took a deep breath and continued. 'Not for days, but for months. Then I read this paper one day. That was the day that I realised what I had done to you, Dev, what everyone you talk about caring for right now had done to you.'

Tears of remorse flowed down her cheeks, her face turned red in anger, in disappointment, not sure for whom.

Dev picked up the paper lying on the table and opened it. It had a few lines on it, a poem; maybe the last one he had written before he lost his memory.

*I need some light, I need some air*

*Distances small, a hand of care*

*I need some smiles, and a drop of tear*

*madness crackling, some anger, some fear*

*I need some thoughts, I need some words*

*I need no flair, I dream no sheen*

*all I want to be is Dev Sareen*

'I would've thrown it away the way I threw away all your other requests, had you given it to me when we were together. I only opened it because you had left, because you hadn't come back.' Kriti turned her face away from him. 'I wanted you back, but I am not sure whether I deserved you. I am not sure if any of us did.'

Kriti took another deep breath and continued, 'You are the best person I have ever met, Dev. Someone who made me feel so special that I forgot that I was an ordinary girl. I think that's what you did to people. You managed to keep everyone so happy, so content that we got used to it. Those who laugh with everyone, often cry alone, Dev. We always saw you happy keeping us happy; we forgot you might cry sometimes as well; I forgot. We were so spoilt by you, Dev. But it is not our fault completely. You are really good at reading people. It was always easy for you to know what was in my mind or your parents', but you never told us you expected the same from us, that you wanted your individuality; you never told us. Then again, it was our fault. I never asked you, nor did your mom. We were a little too happy with your love; we refused to look at all those sacrifices that you were making for us. I think I had become a little too greedy. I didn't realise when I crossed the limit to lose my credibility in your eyes, to lose your confidence in me.'

'Did that give me the right to...'

'No, it didn't,' Kriti didn't let him complete. 'But you were tired of towing the line. There is nothing wrong with taking charge of your life, Dev, but we didn't like that; I didn't like that. I was so used to you following my lead that it was hard for me to accept that it was not going to happen anymore. *That* gave you the right. Yes, that gave you the right.'

Kriti blinked. 'I was trying to protect you. You were too precious, too innocent. I didn't see you stepping up. I didn't realise that what I thought were stupid things were your values, your principles, your style, your view; those things made you Dev Sareen. Everyone failed to see that, Dev. We all failed to see it – your parents, me, your friends, everyone, except Neeti. We were the only people you needed protection from and that is what *she* did. She tried to protect you from us,' Kriti sighed. 'You know how we met Dev?'

'How?'

'Around four years back, you had come to my college to participate in a debate. I was representing my school and you were leading your team. You had delivered a stupendous speech that day. I fell in love with you the moment I heard those lines.'

'What was it?'

'A man is a house of shadows,' she said. 'When you walk in broad daylight, or when you sit beneath a street lamp, or even when you cross the road in front of numerous headlights roaring at you, your shadows remain fearless. There can be one, two or multiple shadows of a person – taller, smaller, fat, skewed, but all his own. It's an easy choice to become one of those shadows and live, but it takes a lot of courage to be the man standing between; the man, who is fearful, yet unperturbed, unchanged, irrespective of whether there is light or not,' Kriti sighed. 'You were a different shadow with me, Dev, a different one with your family and maybe another one with your friends.' A wan smile graced her face, before fading as she continued. 'Neeti might be the only person who has seen the real Dev standing between those shadows and you are the only one who can bring him out to all of us. I hated you for so long for being so ruthless with me and the others who once didn't even matter to me, but only till I realised that people who were happy to be with your shadow never really deserved your love. I was one of those people.'

She paused again. 'I came here because I know I should be the one to apologise. I am responsible, in some way, for what you are today. I don't want you to repeat those mistakes and maybe Neeti didn't either.'

Kriti stood up to walk outside. 'What I have said today wouldn't have made any sense to you, had she not put you through that pain.'

She took her purse from the table and turned towards the door. Dev walked with her to the street. He was lost in thought, so was she.

'Next time we meet, I will see that girlfriend of yours as well,' she smiled and walked away saying, 'be happy, Dev…'

# *Chapter 31*

Dev stood still at the gate for some time; the paper in his hand hung loose in his fingers.

It had been an hour since Kriti had left. He still could not believe that his former girlfriend, the woman who should have felt most wronged by what Neeti had done, was the one defending her actions. He did not know whether he felt like the betrayed or the betrayer. He thought of Neeti. Of Bhawna. His parents. His actions from the time he had woken up alone in that hospital bed, seen that woman in red who had taken him in…

Since Kriti had left, Dev was recalling all those days, those moments spent with Neeti; today he was contemplating the new life she had been trying so hard to give him. He walked to his room and shut the door and took out the thick file one more time.

Dev opened the file and started reading once again. Truth lies in the mind, not in the words because what was written was the same, but the pages held a different perspective this time.

Dev was able to see what he had failed to before. Those pages were not a master plan or a list of complaints against Dev. It was a diary, but not Neeti's. She had been writing down her moments with Dev. It was Dev, who was complaining to her about his life; those moments might have brought disappointment to others, but it was Dev who had felt the pain the most.

'This is not my bible. This is yours,' he whispered, realising for the first time that he had violated Neeti's trust.

Dev was never meant to open that diary. It was meant to provide guidance, but not to him. It was for Neeti to guide Dev, to help him achieve his dreams, to stop him from repeating the same mistakes, to give her the strength to be with him no matter what happened. Dev flung the file back in his bag, disgusted at what he had done to the one person who had always stood by him and opened the door; it was as if he had finally woken up.

'Papa,' he ran to the other room. 'Papa?' He called again.

'Dev,' Mr. Sareen came out of his room.

Mrs. Sareen and Bhawna came out of the kitchen, hearing the urgency in his voice.

Dev looked at the three people standing in front of him. He knew it was hard, but he knew this was the only chance, the only chance to do what he had actually wanted to all those months ago before fate had intervened and left him in a hospital bed, his past forgotten but never far from him.

'I won't go away without saying anything this time,' he said, looking at his mother. 'I am going away. I am leaving again.'

'Where are you going?' Mr. Sareen held his hand.

'To see Neeti, back to the life I have come from. I am going back to Mumbai.'

'Dev!' his mother shouted, 'you are going to meet that witch?'

'Yes.'

'I forbid it. You will not go. You are not going anywhere,' his mother shouted.

'What has happened to you, Dev?' Bhawna asked, her eyes startled, face shocked.

'I don't know,' he turned to Mr. Sareen, 'but I feel only you will understand.' He held his father's hand and kept the sheet of paper in it. 'I am not leaving forever, but I am not going to stop now either.'

Dev turned and walked to his room. He closed the door along with all the tears, noise; people looking at him hopefully, like wounded puppies. He took his bag and left the house.

Mr. Sareen turned the paper in his hand; it was the same poem Kriti had left with Dev.

'Dev.'

Bhawna ran after him as he reached the main door of his house. He turned with a stoic face; his eyes had a confidence Bhawna had failed to see before.

She stopped near him and held his hand.

'What has happened? Are you leaving me here?'

'No, I am just trying to drive away,' Dev said. 'Come with me, but understand that you will have to accept that the girl you hate is a part of my life, a very important part.'

Dev looked at Bhawna's startled face, his eyes calm.

The smile on his face grew larger as he realised something – he had just made another memory for Neeti to note down in her diary.

# *Chapter 32*

'Coming,' Neeti shouted, as the person at the door kept ringing the doorbell again and again.

Neeti rushed to the door barefoot and opened it. There was a bag kept outside. She stood still, surprised. Then she stepped up and carried the bag inside her apartment, leaving the door open.

'I am not going to come out and take you in, Dev,' she shouted, throwing the bag inside his room.

'You aren't curious? Don't you want to know what happened? Why I am here?' Dev said from behind her.

Neeti turned. He was smiling, still at the threshold. She opened the refrigerator and took out the water bottle.

She threw the bottle towards him with teary eyes, still not saying a word. The question evident on her face. Dev caught the bottle and walked to the kitchen.

'I am sorry,' he said.

'I am not looking for a boyfriend,' Neeti clarified, her voice low. 'In case you've come back thinking the same.'

'No,' Dev hugged her before she could cry, let her grief spill over. 'I finally realise. That is the one difference between all of them and you. You refuse to take control of my life even when I try to offer it to you. You don't want a boyfriend or son; you just want me to be Dev and I feel that I want him to be so too.'

Dev took a determined breath and continued. 'It's only after coming back to life again that you realise that you had died once. Living life and being alive are not the same. I want to be alive now. I want to do all the things that I hadn't done before, the things that I don't remember, the things for which I left my home. I know nothing of that Dev, but Kriti helped to meet that Dev again, made me understand why I had left. All you were trying to do was shield me from the pain, warning me not to look back, because that was what I wanted, and I doubted you. Never again. And that's why I've come back. To be free, to live again.'

He kissed her on the forehead and took the knife from her hand.

'So what are we cooking today?'

Dev started peeling an onion as if the past few days had never happened, certain that things were back to normal. He just knew that after everything, Neeti would never let him down, even when he was being a jerk.

Sure enough, Neeti smiled. 'I have already cooked something. But we'll manage.'